To my grandchildren, I have seen many technological advances in my lifetime.

I can only imagine what you will see in yours.

A dedication to you the reader, without you this book would only be a bundle of words, it is imagination that makes any book come to life, use yours while you read this book.

I hope you enjoy.

Brian Johnston

THE LECTURE DIARIES

AUSTIN MACAULEY PUBLISHERS™

LONDON • CAMBRIDGE • NEW YORK • SHARJAH

A CIP catalogue record for this title is available from the British Library.

ISBN 9781398467842 (Paperback)
ISBN 9781398467859 (Hardback)
ISBN 9781398467866 (ePub e-book)

www.austinmacauley.com

First Published 2022
Austin Macauley Publishers Ltd®
1 Canada Square
Canary Wharf
London
E14 5AA

Thanks to Austin Macauley Publishers and their graphics department.

Foreword

As promised the following is a continuation of the previous lecture, but also a separate lecture from last year, this time we are, mainly, concentrating on the diaries of the two crew members who decided to stay on this planet rather than return home with their shipmates. The diaries are in their own words so they can retain their honesty and morality, which this particular species values to a very high degree. Some entries may shock you, some you may find funny, others are controversial. Whatever you decide to take from this, remember to keep an open mind that anything is possible.

Chapter One

It was a beautiful morning in the suburbs of Washington, Dan got in the shower as Lisa went downstairs to prepare breakfast. When Dan came downstairs, Lisa said, "Are you looking forward to today, Dear?"

Dan replied, "Well, I think it's going to be a little different from last year, Honey." After breakfast, Daniel gave Lisa a big kiss and said, "See you tonight, Honey."

"Have a great day," Lisa replied.

Daniel made his way to his car, which was parked in their driveway. He got in the car and put the window down and the radio on to hear the news. As Dr Daniel Brown drove the twenty-five miles to the auditorium, he remembered making the same journey exactly one year before. This time was going to be rather different, Dan thought as he drove along. When Daniel reached the university, there was a designated parking space for him. As he had arrived five minutes early, Daniel took a stroll on the university grounds to enjoy the sunshine before entering the hall. Daniel saw lots of people entering the auditorium, most of whom he recognised from last year. Also, most of them, he already knew.

At precisely three minutes to nine, Dr Daniel Brown entered the auditorium through the large double doors and made his way along the long corridor then, through the double doors and into the main hall. As Dan entered the main hall, he looked around the audience, most of the people were already seated as he made his way to the steps at the side of the stage then, up the steps and to the podium at the centre of the stage, just as it had been one year before.

At precisely nine am on that Monday morning in mid-July, Dr Daniel Brown began to speak.

"Good morning, Ladies and Gentlemen, and thank you for coming; all of you were here last year, and I trust you all did enjoy the lecture and investigation which we did then, as you are all back this year. I did promise you last year to provide future lectures and reports following on from last year's exploits, however, since we covered most of the important points in last year's lecture, we shall not be going over old ground, we shall, in fact, be moving on to something totally new. What I am about to tell you will no doubt totally shock you as you know, we received a visit from a group of alien neighbours one year ago."

"However, what you do not know is that two of the alien visitors decided that they would like to remain on earth for the rest of their lives. That is exactly what has happened."

At this revelation, there was a series of loud conversations within the auditorium. Dan allowed them to digest the information, then continued.

"One male crew and one female crew have remained on earth. They now live here permanently. However, their existence must forever remain a total secret. No one can ever know that they are living on this planet. I will explain the reasons for this in more detail later. When they told me that they wished to live on this planet, I asked them both a couple of weeks later if they could keep diaries, recording their progress and events within their new lives here on earth. They both agreed to provide detailed progress reports, provided they were permitted to speak in their own words with absolutely no alterations. If you remember from last year, these species possess an intense regime of morality and honesty, so if their diaries were to be edited by someone else, this would be contrary to their moral beliefs. I will apologise in advance to anyone who is offended by any of the diary entries as I have read some of their diaries, and som3e entries are, to say the least, rather obscure and graphic."

"This again is due to their rigorous honesty and morality if they did not tell the whole truth and leave out something, this they would consider being the sin of omission, which in their minds would also constitute a lie, and would in effect, breach their moral code. However, their individual perceptions are still subject to their own empirical experiences, but, as always, no matter which planet you hail from, deductive reasoning can always have the capability to be flawed."

"The two crew members decided to live apart in separate houses, as they were not a couple, this would allow them to pursue more normal lives. I would at this time like to extend my thanks to those of you who have made this possible. You know who you are; I do not need to name names. Now, you know what the money I asked you for a year ago was for your trust and generosity is greatly appreciated, as I did not know where I would get access to that kind of cash to buy a couple of houses. So, thank you so much again. The two crew members extend their thanks to you also. I had to tell them where the money came from to buy their new homes. So, let's move on, the following is a graphic description of two lives adapting to a new world, new rules, and a new environment. As I said, some of what you are about to hear may shock you; there will, of course, be time for questions at the end of the presentations. The earth names the two crew have chosen for themselves are Zoe and Ben. I shall begin by presenting to you, excerpts from Zoe's diary as we say here on earth, ladies first."

Chapter Two
Zoe's Diary

Dear diary, this is how Dr Brown said we should begin, we have never encountered these diaries before. My name is Zoe I have decided to remain on this planet rather than return home. The reason being, yes, our world is idyllic and morally correct, but I find this world very interesting with all of its deviations and different ways of life. To describe myself, I am forty-five years old, but look around twenty-five of your earth years old. I have long blond hair and blue eyes, Daniel said I look like a model, but he didn't say that in front of Lisa. I think Daniel and Lisa are a lovely couple and I have a good rapport with both , we could not have met a nicer couple to help us with the transition to our new life on earth. The houses Daniel bought for me and Ben are around three miles apart, they are both lovely with nice pools, gardens and lots of space. More importantly, for us, they both have their own gymnasiums.

On the earth calendar, it is July 24th I have set my day out already, starting with meditation, then a swim in my pool, followed by a workout in the gym, then a five-mile run. Daniel and Lisa have introduced me to a few of their female friends, who have invited me out for an evening with them in a couple of weeks. This, I am looking forward to as I really like meeting new people and making new friends Also, it will give me a chance to see how the other half live, albeit be it on another planet. The story is that I am a distant cousin of Lisa's who has moved here from another state. Daniel said that we probably wouldn't be able to get jobs as we didn't have the proper credentials, I don't know how he's managed it, and I didn't ask, but we now have photo identity cards. Later today, I'm going down to the local mall to try and secure a job in a local hardware store as a shop assistant. Daniel has advised me what to say if they should ask any awkward questions, which I doubt.

I just say, "Sorry, but that's none of your business." I did say to Daniel, "Is that not a bit rude?"

But Daniel said, "Not at all; there is no harm in standing your ground, some people are just nosey, and you are entitled to your privacy."

Once I had my swim, then a workout, and went for a run, it was nearly time for me to go to the interview for my new job. I took a bus down to near the local mall where my job interview was to take place, the mall was quite busy, but I found the shop no bother I had been told to ask for the manager when I arrived, which I did.

After a few minutes, a fat man appeared. He said, "Hi, you must be Zoe."

I said, "I am, indeed. How do you do?"

"I'm very good, thanks, come with me, please." He then led me to an office at the rear of the shop. "Please take a seat; welcome to Jack's hardware."

"Thanks," I said.

"My name is Mike, by the way," he said.

"This won't take long. I just have a few questions for you if that's okay, to see if you're suitable for the job; have you worked in a hardware shop before?"

"Nope, I've never worked in any shop before," I said.

"I have to say you are very beautiful. You could be a model," said Mike.

"I don't want to be a model; I just want a job in a hardware shop," I said with a big smile.

"Okay, you have the job," said Mike, "we'll give you a month's trial, you can pick it up as you go along. We work from nine to five; it's Friday now, so, we won't throw you in at the deep end. If you can be here at 8:45 am on Monday, I'll get someone to show you the ropes before the store opens."

"Thank you! I'll see you on Monday morning at 8:45 sharp."

When I had been home for a short while, Daniel called my mobile phone, "Hi, how did the interview go?"

"Hi, great," I said. "I got the job, apparently, I will be in charge of the ropes."

"Ropes?" Daniel said.

"Yes," I said, "I have to be there at 8:45 sharp on Monday morning for someone to show me the ropes."

Daniel started laughing, "That's just an expression, Zoe," he said. "That just means to show you how the store operates."

"Oh, I see! There will probably be a lot of these expressions I will have to get used to over time."

"Don't worry, you'll get there, Zoe," said Daniel.

The rest of the day, I just swam in my pool and sunbathed. The weather here is lovely, much the same as in my home world, with constant sunshine and warmth. The following day, Saturday, we had arranged to go to a show which was on, at the local theatre, with Daniel, Lisa, and a few of their friends. It was a very good show, although the language was a bit alien to us. This play was by someone called Shakespeare. Lisa had said that even she had had trouble understanding some of the dialogue. After the show, we all mingled in the garden at Daniel and Lisa's house for a while, then we all made our way home.

Ben and I got a cab. He dropped me off first as my house was on the way to his. On the way home, Ben said, "What do you think of it so far?"

I said that I quite liked it. I told him I had secured a job in a hardware store in a local mall and asked if he had done anything about getting a job yet. Ben had always been good with mechanical stuff and said he was going to try and get a job in a local garage; this he would enjoy, and it would keep him fit at the same time. The next day, it was a beautiful Sunday morning, July 26th, my day began with a meditation and a swim, as usual, then a workout and a run.

This afternoon, I am attending a barbecue at one of the girl's houses, who I am going out with soon. Ben is also invited, as are Daniel and Lisa. I am looking forward to this as I enjoy meeting new people. After we had been there for around an hour, we were all standing around the pool area in the garden, suddenly I felt a hard slap on my bottom, really hard. "Hi, you must be Zoe. I'm John. How are you doing?"

"Oh, really," I said. I moved my glass from my right hand to my left and proceeded to punch him square on the jaw. We were standing beside the swimming pool, which he landed in, "Do not ever put your hands on me again, or next time, you will get hurt much worse," I said.

"Hey, I was only being friendly," he said.

"That's not friendliness, that's a perversion," I said. "Don't ever put your fucking hands on me again." I had learnt this was an appropriate expression when you are angry.

Daniel came running over and asked, "Zoe are you okay?"

"Yes, I'm fine, thanks, Daniel, I did not think you would have friends like these."

Daniel said, "John, what the hell are you doing?"

He replied, "It wasn't meant in a bad way."

Then, the girl whose party it was came running over – Kate said, "Okay, John, you can remove yourself from my pool, thank you, then you can remove yourself from my house."

Hearing this, he then shouted at me saying, "Look at the trouble you've caused."

As he was climbing out of the pool, I went over; and side kicked him square in the chest, "Don't ever put your hands on me," I said. "And don't ever talk to me like that again, now, is there anything else you would like to say, John?" I spoke. He said nothing, got out of the pool on the other side and left.

Kate said, "I am so sorry about him, he split up with his wife a few months ago, and he has been desperately trying to find a woman since then."

"That's no way to go about it," I said.

After that incident, everyone just enjoyed the rest of the evening; the food was delicious, the conversation was stimulating, and the company was very pleasant. Then around 10:30 pm, we all heard, kind of like a roar. Then, out of the shadows, appeared John; he was absolutely drunk.

John started to make his way towards me, and Ben looked over and gestured as in, would I be, okay? I just smiled with one side of my mouth raised as in, no problem. John made his way towards me as he got closer, I never moved an inch. His speech was so slurred, he said or tried to say, "I would just like to say that you are the most beautiful woman I have ever seen in my life. I am very sorry for my behaviour earlier; please forgive me."

I said, "Well done John, okay, you're forgiven, but don't ever put your hands on me again."

At that, he collapsed on the grass a few feet in front of me, "Ben, give me a hand with this, would you?" I spoke. We picked him up, took him to the front of the house, and called a cab. Luckily, Kate knew his address, and luckily again, the cab driver took him home.

The music was playing loud, and everyone was dancing and having a great time, as they say here, when in Rome do as the Romans. Ben and I partook in a few alcoholic beverages – something we would never have done in our home world. The feeling was so strange, and to be honest, I really did not like it at all. I started to feel rather ill. Ben said he felt the same so, that was the end of our experience with alcohol, or so I thought.

The next morning, thankfully, I was feeling a bit better as I was to start my new job. I arrived at the shop at 8:45 am as arranged and waited for some guidance as to what to do next. After a few moments, a girl came over and said, "Hi, you must be Zoe. I'm Lucy. How are you doing?"

"Hi, yes, that's right. I'm Zoe, I'm fine, thanks," I said.

Lucy was around forty years old, with long brown hair and hazel eyes; she was not unattractive. She was well-built and looked very sturdy. "Well, aren't you a pretty little thing," she said. "Why, the fuck, do you want to work in a hardware shop for?" she asked.

I was a bit confused, she didn't seem angry, but she was using the "fuck" word. I decided just to go with the flow so, I said, "I just fancied a fucking change."

Lucy asked, "Oh, yeah, what did you do before?"

I blurted out, "I was a pilot, fuck, I mean, I was in a pilot for a TV show, but it didn't work out."

"Ah, I see, so you thought you'd come and grab a screw or two and twist a few nuts," Lucy said, laughing.

Now, I was really confused, "Yes, I said, that is correct."

Lucy looked a bit confused now also, "Okay, Kid, follow me," she said. Lucy told me they had just received a large delivery, and everything had to be unpacked and put on display on the various shelves.

I said, "Yes, that's no problem. I can do that." It was quite heavy work, but I enjoyed it; it was just like another work out.

At 5 pm, Mike popped his head out of the office and shouted, "Okay, guys, that's time for today." That was the time the shop closed for the day.

Lucy came over to me and said, "Hey Kid, do you fancy going out for a beer with me?"

"Yes, sure," I said, "I'll just have a soft drink if you don't mind. I had a few yesterday, and I'm still suffering."

"No worries," Lucy said, "We'll go to my local; it's just around the corner."

I said, "Okay."

When we got to the bar, which wasn't far away as we walked into the bar, one girl shouted and whistled at the same time, "Hey, Lucy, Love, who's the new catch."

Lucy replied, "Shut the fuck up, this is a new workmate of mine; her name is Zoe."

"Hey, Zoe," they all shouted in turn.

"Hi," I said. After a couple of drinks, I said to Lucy, "Lucy, for this to be a bar, there aren't many or any men in it."

Lucy said laughing, "Sweetie, it's a gay bar, you know, lesbian, does that bother you?"

"No, not at all." I had heard of this before but never encountered it yet.

Lucy said, "I take it, you're not gay?"

"No, I'm not. I prefer a male-female union; did you think I was?" I asked.

Lucy said, "Well, you can never tell; lots of beautiful girls prefer a female-to-female relationship."

I said, "Do you have a girlfriend, Lucy?"

"Well, I did until a couple of weeks ago. We had lived together for five years, then she met someone she liked better and left."

"I'm so sorry; do you miss her very much?"

"Well, I suppose I do a bit. It's different going home to an empty house after work and waking up on your own in the mornings."

"Do you still see her?" I asked.

"Yes, we're still on speaking terms I see her and her new partner all the time when I'm out and about," Lucy replied.

Just at that, the door to the bar opened, and two females walked in. "Oh fuck, speak of the devil," Lucy said. One of the females had long blond hair and was quite slim; the other had dark brown hair and was a bit chunkier. They went to the bar to order a drink, they looked around, and saw Lucy. When they got their drinks, they came over to the table where we were sitting.

The blond said to Lucy, "Hi, how are you?"

Lucy replied, "I'm good, cheers; how are you?"

The blond replied, "I'm good, thanks; who's your new friend?"

Lucy said, "It's none of your business, and we are having a private conversation, so, goodbye."

At that, the two went and sat at another table.

"Is everything okay?" I said to Lucy.

Lucy replied, "Yeah, fuck her, she has always been a jealous bitch, so I hope she is seething with jealousy now."

At this revelation, my immediate thoughts were, *am I actually being used to create these jealous feelings?*

"Well, I've enjoyed the drinks, but I have to get going now, Lucy."

Lucy said, "You can't leave me sitting here on my own with her over there. I'll look stupid."

I realised I had been used to invoke these jealous feelings in the girl, "I have to get going, Lucy," I said.

"Okay, I'll come out with you," Lucy said.

We walked out of the bar, giving everyone the impression we were a couple.

Once outside, I said, "Lucy, can I ask you a question, and will you as answer me honestly?"

"Go ahead, ask away, Kid."

"Did you ask me to come to the bar with you to portray to your ex that you were now in another relationship?"

"Okay, you got me; there's no harm in that, though, is there?"

"Well, yes, I'm afraid there is, Lucy. I thought we may have become friends, but the moral ethic which you have displayed tells me that you will use anyone to achieve your own goals in effect, you used me, Lucy."

"Aww, you can go fuck yourself," Lucy said, to which I replied, "When I decide to enter into a union, I will allow the man I am in union with to do that for me, thank you."

Lucy said, "Come on, I didn't mean any harm."

"Perhaps, you should consider your actions more carefully in the future, no doubt. I shall see you at the shop tomorrow, goodnight," I said.

Chapter Three

The next morning, I arrived at the shop at 8:45. At 9 am, I continued doing what I had been doing the day before. After around twenty minutes, Lucy walked in a bit late; she came straight over to me and said, "I am sorry about last night; can we just forget it and have a fresh start?"

It was only my second day on the job, and I knew we had to work together, so I just said, "Sure, no worries," but I knew I would never trust her again. As I settled into, what was now my working week, I had to re-arrange my swim and workout schedule. What used to happen in the mornings now took place in the evenings; this was better for me, though, as it filled my whole day and night. I liked working in the shop as there was quite a variety of things to learn and do.

As I was working today, Thursday the 30th of July, I was filling shelves when I saw a young man who appeared to be wearing work trousers, with big pockets on the sides. However, I saw him fill several pockets with screws and nails. I didn't think much of it at the time. I thought he was just going to the checkout and then paying for them. Then, I realised what he was, I had heard about these but had never actually seen one before, he was a shoplifter. I thought to myself. *He's not going to steal our merchandise.* As I watched him, it became more and more clear that he was trying to get as much as possible into his pockets and then run out of the shop. I walked around the top of the aisle where he was and picked up a basket. I then walked around and down the aisle where he was and said, "Would you like a basket for all that, Sir?"

He said, "All that? I haven't picked anything up yet."

Oh dear, I thought, *a shoplifter and a liar.* "Then, what's all the hardware in your pockets," I said.

"That's just screws and nails from a job I'm working on," he said.

"OK, in that case, I will let you continue shoplifting."

At this remark, he looked totally surprised. I smiled and started to walk away. Then, I stopped and said, "Oh, and can you please follow me to the office at the rear of the store, Sir, you are our one-millionth customer today, and I have a surprise for you."

"I don't want it," he said.

"But it's lots of money," I said.

"I don't want it," he said.

"But Sir, it will enable you to pay for all the stolen goods you have in your pockets."

At this, he started walking backward. I walked forwards towards him; he turned and started to run but nowhere near as quickly as me. I put his arm up to his back and marched him up to Mike's office, knocked on the door, opened it, and said, "Shoplifter, Mike." The shoplifter was a big guy and was trying to get loose, but my grip on his arm was too strong.

"Will you tell her to get the fuck off me," he said to Mike. "Nah, I think she's doing just fine," said Mike, "so, you think your gonna steal from my store, huh?" said Mike.

"Come on, Man, give me a break. I was desperate."

"I am gonna give you a break," said Mike, "a jailbreak, you're going to jail, Boy," Mike called the police, and they arrived within about half an hour, two officers came into the shop and to the office at the back of the shop.

One officer said, "Well done! we've been after him for a while. He's been stealing from all of the shops in the mall."

"I've got my new start to thank."

"Really," a policeman said, "what's his name?"

Mike said, "He's a *she*, Zoe, that's her down that aisle."

"Wow, she's a pretty girl," one policeman said, "OK, if we go and have a word."

Mike said, "Yes, sure."

"Excuse me, Miss; I believe you are the one who apprehended the shoplifter."

"I am indeed," I said, "I'm not having that in our store."

One officer said, "Can I ask, do you have a boyfriend, or are you single?"

"I am single at the moment," I said, "why do you ask?"

"Oh, I just wondered if you might like to go for a meal or a drink sometime?"

I told him that I didn't drink much, but yes, we could go for a meal or a drink. He asked if he could get my phone number, I told him, and he put it into his phone.

"I'm Zak, by the way, I'll give you a call, and we can go out some time if you like."

"I'd like that," I said, "not this weekend, though, as I have plans already."

"OK, I'll call you next week," he said. Then, they took the shoplifter away in the police car.

"That should be the last we see of him," said Mike, "well done, you!" he said to me.

Saturday, August 1st, well, that was my first week at work and it was quite eventful. I'm going out with the girls tonight. I've been told we are going to a few cocktail bars and a club. We don't really do this in my home world, so I phoned Kate and asked her what I should wear. She said, usually, a little black cocktail dress never fails to look good. I arranged to meet her in town this afternoon. So that we can go shopping, and I can pick one up. I'm looking forward to this as it's all new to me, I'm quite excited about tonight, but in the meantime, I'm off to go shopping in town.

Well, diary, that was an eventful couple of hours, I met Kate at 2 pm as arranged, and we made our way around several shops to see if I could find a dress I liked. There are a few malls in town, and Kate said we should go into this one as it had some great dress shops, so, we did. While looking around the shops, I started to get the feeling I was being watched, then the reason for this became apparent. "Well, fancy seeing you here," as I turned around, I saw there were three men directly behind myself and Kate – "this is the little bitch that got me jailed on Thursday," the one in the middle said.

"It's the shoplifter I had caught a couple of days before," I said to Kate; she had probably better get security; she moved away slowly at first then started to run.

"Yeah, you're a real pretty little thing, aren't you? I think I'm gonna change that right now," he said. He then produced a knife from his back pocket, pressed a button on the handle, and the blade flicked out.

"You're a very silly man," I told him, "if you try to hurt me with that, you are the one who will be seriously hurt." He looked surprised that I wasn't frightened or didn't try to run away; he made a stabbing gesture to try and scare me. I adopted a defensive stance. He made another stabbing gesture, and I grabbed his arm and put it in an arm lock; both I and Ben are extremely highly trained in combat situations. He was much bigger than me. I am around 5 ft 4 inches, and this man was around 6 ft 2 inches. While I had his arm in a lock, one of his friends tried to intervene. I kicked him in the head, then both of them ran off. I then side-kicked the shoplifter in the knee, and he went down to the ground; he started moaning in pain, "I told you, *you* would get hurt," I said.

Two security guards came running over at that point. There were also two policemen running into the mall from another direction. One policeman said, "What's going on here?" while the other one handcuffed the shoplifter. I told them I had caught him stealing in our shop a couple of days earlier and that he had pulled a knife out when he saw me here. By this time, they had radioed in and figured out who the guy was.

The policeman said, "He was on bail from two days before, but now he will go straight to jail to await his trial. You won't see him again for a long time, Miss; carrying a knife is a serious offence, he will get a long prison sentence for that, threatening someone with it is even worse."

"The fact that he went to attack you with it means he will be charged with anything from serious assault to attempted murder."

"Well done to you, Miss!" one policeman said, "he might have attacked someone less able to defend themselves than you."

Kate was a bit shaken up by this time. "Let's go for a coffee," I said, "then we'll do some more shopping."

After we had had a coffee and eventually picked up my outfit for the evening, Kate dropped me off at home in a cab, and we arranged to go shopping again next weekend. I told her that I would see her at the cocktail bar this evening as I was going to Lisa's first, and we were heading out together. I had my shower and finished getting ready. I felt great in my new flimsy black silk underwear and my new little black cocktail dress. I am now going to head to Lisa's, and we'll leave from there for a night out with the girls. I will provide a full report on the events of the evening tomorrow.

Good morning, Diary, fuck, my head hurts. I decided to give the alcohol experience another chance. I took a cab to Lisa's last night as arranged around 7 pm. Dan answered the door and instantly said, "Wow, you look stunning. Come on in and get a drink; are you still on the orange juice?" he asked.

"Yes, I am, Daniel."

We had a few drinks and a chat in the garden, then Lisa and I got a cab to the cocktail bar where we had arranged to meet the rest of the girls. They were mostly all there by the time we got there, "just a couple more to appear," Lisa said. She introduced me to all the girls in turn; there were eight of us in all. "I'll get us a drink," said Lisa, "would you like an orange juice?"

"Actually, no," I said, "I think I'm going to try some of these cocktails; they look delicious," I told Lisa.

She looked surprised and said, "OK, but remember they are very strong."

The first one I had was called a 'Virgin's Downfall,' it was delicious and just like drinking juice. All the girls were chatting away about their working week and their families; four of them were married, a few asked me which modelling agency I was with, I told them that I'm not a model. I work in a hardware shop; they just said, "Oh!" The next cocktail I tried was called 'Sex on the Beach.' I said quietly to Lisa, "I knew this one as I had had a couple of unions in my home world, where this had actually occurred."

Lisa let out a brief, loud single laughing noise; she said, "Oh really, Madam, thank you for your honesty; can I ask how long did these unions last?"

"Oh, it was only for one night," I said, none of the other girls could hear our conversation.

Lisa said, "We have those types of unions on this planet too; they are called one-night stands, but to be honest, the types of girls who indulge in these don't create a very good image for themselves."

I said, "But what about all the freedom you have with all the deviations in your world? Is this not too acceptable?"

Lisa said, "Not really; it can also be very dangerous; there are lots of sexually transmitted diseases going around, and you can never be sure who has what, and some are incurable." Lisa said that she thought I would benefit from a long conversation with Daniel on this subject; she said she would speak to him tomorrow and get him to call me. Lisa and Daniel were very kind to both me and Ben; they totally looked after us, then it was time for my next cocktail. Lisa said, "Maybe, I shouldn't mix so many drinks."

I said, "It's OK, I have a strong metabolism," or so I thought. We went to several more bars, and various guys tried to chat me up. Lisa had said that I would get a lot of that because I was so pretty. Later around 1 am, the bars were closing, and we went to a club; the music was unbelievably loud the place was full. One of the doormen tried to chat me up, but I was just nice to him and said what Lisa had told me to say, "I'm in a relationship," I said, "I have been for some time." I know we don't normally lie due to our rigorous moral convictions, but this was an exceptional circumstance, and there was no real harm being done so, on this occasion, it was acceptable.

As the night went on, we all just danced and had a great time; there were a few fights that broke out in the club, but the doormen were good and came right to the scene of any trouble. One of the girls who wasn't married met a guy and left the club with him; she said goodnight to everyone before she left. Lisa said, "She's OK; she isn't drunk. She knows what she is doing, and I know her well; she is not the type to have a one-night stand."

The girls who were married, seemed to get a lot more drunk than the rest of us did This, I did not understand. I had thought that it would have been the other way around. As we left the club, Lisa said, "Would you like a burger?"

"That would be great," I said, "where do we get one?" I asked.

"Just around here," at that, we turned the corner, and a burger stall was visible just down the street. It was 3 am by this time. We ate our burgers while waiting in the taxi rank, "That was the best burger I have had in a long time," I said to Lisa.

I dropped Lisa off home and then headed to my house; it was around 3:45 am when I eventually got home. I went straight to sleep as I was quite drunk by this time; hence, my head was hurting so much this morning, I think I will leave and go for my swim for a while. Suffice to say that it was a good night. I learned quite a lot and met lots of nice people.

Chapter Four

Dear, Diary, later this afternoon, my mobile rang; it was Daniel, he said, "Hi," and asked how I was. I said that I was fine and that my head was returning to normal now, after my alcohol experience last night. Daniel said that he wanted to chat with me, so he and Lisa would come over to my house tomorrow evening, around 6:30 pm.

"Yes, of course," I had told him, "Is there anything wrong?" I asked.

But Daniel said, "No, not at all, I have promised to look after you guys, and it's just an update on your progress here on earth."

I told Daniel that I looked forward to seeing him and Lisa tomorrow night, and that I would prepare some snacks and drinks.

Monday morning, the start of a fresh week, I got a surprise when I went to work this morning. Mike shouted for me to go into his office at the back of the shop. I thought for a brief moment that I was in some kind of trouble, but on the contrary, I was in for a pleasant surprise. "Take a seat," Mike said as I went into his office, so I sat down. "I'll be back in one minute," he said. When Mike returned to the room, he placed a piece of paper in front of me on the table and said, "Just sign that."

"Oh, I can't sign that," I said, "I have encountered this before, and it's not possible for me to sign."

"What do you mean?" said Mike, "this is only your contract of employment; it means you have a secure job here for a year. Everybody signs one of these, every year. I know that you are such a good worker. I don't need a month to judge if we are going to keep you on or not; you have the job, your trial period is over, well done!"

"Oh, thank you very much!" I said,

"OK, back to work," Mike said. There was a mirror on the back of the door in Mike's office, and I caught sight of Mike apparently looking at my bottom as I got up to leave. Mike was around five years older than me but looked much older; there was absolutely no attraction from my side towards him at all, but I had remembered the "Honey" remark when I had first gone for my interview. I had thought at that time that I would need to watch this one. Mike has never been anything other than a perfect gentleman, and he is married, so I suppose the proper saying on this occasion is that there is no harm in looking. On the positive side, I am very pleased about the contract. I have secured my first full-time job; this will be great news to tell Daniel and Lisa this evening; they should be here shortly; I had better go and get ready.

Dr Brown then said to the audience, "We shall now take a short break; there is tea, coffee, sandwiches, and refreshments in the hall opposite Ladies and Gentlemen; if you would care to help yourselves, we shall resume in around twenty minutes."

After around twenty minutes, the hall started to fill up again; when nearly everyone was seated, Dr Brown made his way to the podium. Daniel began to speak, "Okay, let's continue, guards, if you please." At this remark, the security guards started moving around the auditorium, locking all the doors and securing the exits. There was a lot of turning of heads and mumbling around the hall. Daniel said, "Don't be alarmed, please. I know you have all signed the official secrets act, and you are all sworn to secrecy; this is merely an added precaution due to the sensitive content of what I am about to present to you." Dr Brown took a moment to compose himself and allow the guards to finish securing the hall, then continued, "What I am about to present to you is something totally new, which none of us have ever been privy to before. You may dismiss what I am about to tell you like rubbish and or fabrication, however, you have all met the crew members from the other world and know that their morality and culture are based on rigorous honesty and do not permit lying of any kind."

"Therefore, I guarantee that you will not be able to disprove anything which I am about to present to you, especially as it is in Zoe's own words," Dan continued, "I was actually shocked to hear this myself, but here is what happened when Lisa and I visited Zoe on that Monday evening. I shall now refer back to Zoe's diary."

Good morning, Diary, Tuesday morning, another day, another dollar seems to be a popular expression here in this world. That was quite an eventful evening last night with Daniel and Lisa; they arrived at around 6:30 pm, and I had prepared snacks and drinks in the garden. Daniel began by saying, "Well, Zoe, can I ask, how have you found your first few weeks here on earth?"

I replied, "Yes, Daniel, it has been very enlightening, to say the least so far."

Then Daniel said, "Please don't take this the wrong way; we are only concerned for your wellbeing."

I said, "I know you are, both you and Lisa have been so kind to Ben and me since we arrived, please continue, Daniel; what can I help you with?"

Daniel said, "Well, Zoe, I know about the confrontation with John at the barbecue; after all, I was there. Lisa tells me that there have been a couple of more incidents since then, yes?"

"Sorry, Daniel," I said, "nope, there haven't been any more incidents. I have never seen John since the day of the barbecue."

Daniel smiled and said, "No, Zoe, I don't mean with John, I mean, the Lucy and the shoplifter incidents."

"Oh," I said, "Daniel, I thought you were coming over to talk to me about my 'Sex on the Beach,' in my home world, and these sexually transmitted diseases of yours in this world." I started laughing and said, "I don't mean yours personally, Daniel, obviously." Now, Lisa was laughing as well.

Daniel said, "Yes, we'll talk about that a bit later; for now, though, I would like to talk about the incidents with Lucy and the shoplifter if you don't mind."

"Not at all," I said, "my manager, Mike, was very impressed with my apprehending the shoplifter; in fact, I signed my contract of employment to give me a job for one whole year today."

Lisa said, "That's excellent news, Zoe; well done, you!"

"Yes, well done, Zoe!" Daniel said, "although I am a bit concerned about the attention you are drawing to yourself."

I had to say, "Sorry, Daniel, I don't know what you mean. I have never purposely brought attention to myself."

Daniel said, "I know you didn't do it on purpose, Zoe; the thing is, I would try and avoid future confrontations with shoplifters if I were you. If you combine what happened in the shop and what happened in the mall; these are incidents that make you stand out from the crowd if you know what I mean." Daniel continued, "your existence here on earth is supposed to be and has to remain one of secrecy, but now because of the shoplifter incident you will have to make a court appearance to give evidence," Daniel said, "I am only concerned for your welfare, Zoe."

I said, "Surely, I won't have to go to court. The incident in the mall with the knife was all on camera; he cannot possibly plead not guilty to that."

Daniel said that he could, and he would. He would take every opportunity to try and avoid going to jail.

"Now, I see what you mean, Daniel," I said, "If I become too noticeable and upset too many people, they will, at some point, send me to the next level with an assisted opt-out, yes?" I said to Daniel and Lisa. I was going to ask them about this at another time, but this seemed to be an appropriate time to broach this subject.

Daniel and Lisa looked a bit surprised and bewildered. Daniel said, "Are you feeling okay, Zoe? I must admit I am a bit confused."

"Yes, I am fine, Daniel; let me explain. You see, as well as the enhanced physical abilities we have compared to yourselves, Ben, and I, and indeed, all of our species have enhanced mental abilities compared to yourselves. We are empathic to the point where we can empathise partially with the next level."

Daniel said, "Zoe, are you saying that you and Ben and all of your species are psychics?"

"Well, I suppose you could put it that way; it's not all of the time; it only happens, occasionally, when we meditate."

Daniel said, "Why do you mention this now, Zoe; can I ask?"

I told Daniel that within some of my recent meditations, I had encountered certain essences, combined with some research into his world's history that I had done. I have learned about some of your assisted opt-outs, what you call assassinations. "If I become too noticeable and too bold within your society or upset the wrong people, I could be opted-out with assistance, yes?"

Daniel said, "Well, I suppose that is one way to put it, Zoe."

Daniel then addresses the audience, "Okay, at this point, I am going to intervene for a moment. I think we all know where this is leading; I was as shocked as you probably all are to hear what Zoe was saying." Dan continued, "At this point, this is all purely conjecture. Although Zoe's culture is one based on morality and stringent honesty, I would say, and Zoe and Ben agree, that because there is no concrete or empirical evidence to support any empathic contact with the next level, the statements must be treated as subjective, which is the same with any psychic readings or predictions; there is no concrete empirical evidence to present. I shall now return to the diary entries."

Daniel said that it would be best to keep any empathic experiences about the next level between ourselves that there were enough conspiracy theorists on this planet already.

I said, "I know, Daniel, but I have done a little research into your history, and it appears that your race is very good at creating a smoke screen when you wish to assist someone to the next level."

Daniel said, "Zoe, I suggest you refrain from researching our history; some of it is rather dark and jaded and also very subjective. There are a lot of different conspiracy theories with no tangible evidence to support them."

I said, "I think not, Daniel. I think there are a lot of cover-ups and smoke screens to disguise what has actually happened."

Daniel said, "You will need to be careful, Zoe; what you can say and what you can prove are two totally different things; this is how we got into this discussion in the first place. I cannot stress enough that we need to keep your identity a secret as much as possible. On this occasion, as far as the shoplifter is concerned, I will have a word with a friend of mine; you probably won't need to go to court on this occasion, but please be careful in the future and try not to get involved or noticed."

"Okay, Daniel, I will try, thank you!" I spoke.

Daniel did tell me that he was not being harsh, that he was only looking after my best interests, I told him I knew this, and he had always done so. Daniel continued, "As far as the sexually transmitted diseases we were going to discuss, I was only going to say that after Lisa told me how honest you were on the night out you all had, I thought I had better explain that in this world, we have certain sexually transmittable diseases which are incurable, the main ones being HIV and Hepatitis."

"Zoe, do you have such diseases in your home world, can I ask?" Lisa asked.

I said, "Well, actually no, we don't have these or any other diseases. As soon as one is discovered, any kind of ailment or disease such as these, any ones we couldn't cure with meditations, we then develop a vaccine or a treatment to eradicate the disease."

Daniel then said to the audience, "What Zoe is referring to with curing within meditations is self-healing, another ability which this race possesses, a topic which we shall cover a little later. This next part, I found difficult to comprehend myself, but as I say, due to Zoe's species' rigorous honesty, I cannot doubt what was said next." "Now, we shall return to the diary entries. Also, Zoe knows and has no objections that the diary entries are being presented within this lecture."

"We have had occasion to create new vaccines ourselves within the past couple of years," Daniel said, "because of the Coronavirus, the Covid-19 pandemic, which has spread throughout our world, we also have had to develop vaccines to try and subdue the disease."

I told Daniel I knew about the disease, then asked him if he knew where it had originated. Daniel said, "Well, there are various theories; one rather obscure theory is that a prediction by a prophet from a few hundred years ago, Nostradamus, has come to fruition. He said that evil would descend upon the world in the year 2019. There is a corresponding coincidence to this theory, which is that there are six letters within the word corona and the corresponding places of the six letters within our alphabet are as follows:

C = 3
O = 15
R = 18
O = 15
N = 14
A = 1
6 + 66 = 666

"Combining this other coincidence is an excerpt, from within the book of revelations in our Holy Bible. It is said that the beast shall be known by a number and that number shall be 666, the sign of the beast, the Devil. This is pure supposition, conjecture, and coincidence, I know, but it is a strange coincidence all the same. Another theory is that it has been transmitted from an animal or a bat to a human being. The third theory is that it was an accident within a laboratory in a province in China."

I then said, "And you believe one of these theories to be the cause, Daniel?"

Daniel said, "Well, yes, without any other explanations being offered, there is no option but to accept one of these explanations, which one, I don't know." Then Daniel asked me if I knew something different, which, in fact, I do but, we are limited and were warned before we left our home world about divulging any amount of information regarding other worlds and lifeforms which we know of within the universe, Also regarding if we could or should share information with the population of earth. "Daniel, this is very difficult for me as I cannot lie, and I do know something different. I know many things about the universe which you do not, however, I am limited as to the amount of information which I am permitted to divulge; please try and understand."

Daniel said, "Of course, Zoe, but I know if you knew of a quicker cure you, would tell me, yes?"

I told Daniel, that of course, I would, but the vaccine which his species has developed, will suffice for the present.

"Are you saying there will be further strains of the virus to deal with, Zoe?"

I told Daniel that I didn't know the honest answer to tell. Also, that I was limited to what I could tell and what not as my species is bound by certain rules which prevent us from interfering in other species' growth and outcomes. "What I will say is that do you not think it is strange that as soon as your people developed a vaccine for the original virus, a stronger, deadlier strain then appeared?"

Daniel said to the audience that this statement infers that someone had created this virus, and when we 'fought back,' they created a stronger strain. I had asked Zoe whether I would have been right in saying that. We shall now return to the diary entries.

I told Daniel that since I couldn't lie, yes, he would be quite correct in saying that. Daniel then asked, "Have you then encountered this virus before, Zoe?" I told Daniel that we knew of the virus.

Dr Brown then addressed the audience, "At this point, I will intervene again, If you remember the lecture from last year, we discussed the cause and effects within the universe; what Zoe is saying regarding the effect is that if their species knew of the existence of the coronavirus, this would indicate that the virus is not specific to earth. As I have said on many occasions, you can never have any effect without there being a prior cause in place."

I had then asked Zoe the direct question, "Did this virus originate in yours or another world?"

Her answer was astonishing. We shall now return to the diary entries:

Dear, Diary, when Daniel asked me the question about the virus last night, I could no longer evade the answer, "Yes, Daniel, the virus originated in another world."

Daniel then asked, "But since you are the only other species we have physically encountered within the universe, are you saying that the virus began in your world?"

I told Daniel, "No, not us, and we are not the only species you have encountered."

Lisa then said, "Zoe, please tell us what is going on; this is all becoming very confusing."

"I'm sorry, Lisa. I will tell you, as I say, we are bound by certain protocols when divulging information about the universe, but you and Daniel are so kind to us I cannot refrain from telling you, and I know I can trust you not to say anything to anyone."

Chapter Five

Zoe then began, "This all started long before any of us were born; how good is your history, guys?"

Daniel said, "Well, my knowledge is quite good."

Lisa said, "Mine is probably not as good as Dan's but not too bad."

"As you say, Daniel, the effect is the virus; the cause began seventy-three years ago."

Daniel and Lisa looked at each other totally confused and bewildered. Zoe continued to tell them, "This series of events began in your year, 1945; you mentioned this in your lecture last year, Daniel, do you remember?"

Daniel said, "The only reference to that era was the indiscriminate bombing of the Japanese islands of Hiroshima and Nagasaki."

I said, "Correct, Daniel, the force generated by the nuclear bombs was enough to attract the attention of a small passive species many light-years from this world."

"Although it would have taken them many years to travel to earth, they did have a vessel close enough to earth to investigate the seismic activity. They arrived two years later, in your year, 1947; their mission was one of secrecy and exploration; also, they did not know if there were life forms on this planet, and whether they would be welcomed or attacked."

Daniel then said, "Are you talking about Roswell, New Mexico, Zoe?"

"Yes, Daniel, I am. Do you remember the story and what happened?"

Daniel said, "To my knowledge, it was a weather balloon that went wrong, then there were lots of stories about an alien spaceship crashing, but it was all supposition and conjecture. There was no actual proof of any alien spacecraft."

I said to Daniel, "Another one of the cover-ups we mentioned earlier. Their ship was dissected, and all of the technology cannibalised. Think about the advances your species has made technologically in the last seventy years, Daniel," I continued, "where do you think all of this technology came from?"

Daniel said, "This is fascinating, Zoe; please continue."

"Unfortunately, it was not just their spacecraft, which was dissected; there were also seven crew members aboard the ship. Rather than trying to communicate with them, they were, in effect, taken prisoner, then mutilated and murdered. Absolutely disgusting behaviour. Their home world did not know what had happened to the crew; they just knew that there was no contact with them; they had assumed that their ship had crashed or disintegrated while entering the earth's atmosphere. Then some years later, once you had developed your internet, videos of alien autopsies were being posted on the World Wide Web. The species your race had tortured, mutilated, and murdered was a quiet, non-violent race with no war-like tendencies at all. However, on a future recognisance mission, the horrible truth about what had happened to their comrades was discovered. They had accessed your internet, which was quite easy for them as it was, they who had developed the technology initially. They were horrified with what they saw and once they researched some of human history, the aliens realised that human beings were a barbaric, savage, and arrogant race – whom they would have nothing to do with."

Daniel said, "Zoe, how, can I ask, do you know all of this?"

"Of course, Daniel, I will tell you, as I said before, this race is not aggressive, and they had have never encountered anything like this before. Many years ago, they approached our race and asked for our help. They knew that we had very powerful weapons, and they wanted revenge for what had happened to their people. While we sympathised with them, we could not get involved. Ultimately, this is a very unfortunate incident that has now changed their race forever. What was once a peaceful, non-violent race, is now a race that is seeking vengeance."

"I cannot tell you when they will consider that enough is enough and that their crewmen have been avenged. At the end of the day, you are helpless; their planet is many light-years away, you do not have the technology to go there or even find it; even if you could, you would not be able to communicate with this race, so on this occasion, there is nothing at all you can do."

Daniel said, "Is there no way you can help us, Zoe, to at least request them for no stronger strains of the virus to be released."

I told Daniel that I was sorry, but as I had said before, we couldn't t get involved, the same thing we had told the Greys.

Daniel said, "Is that what they are called?"

I told him that I knew his race had referred to them in this manner before I said, "To be honest, you could not pronounce this species name or speak their language as you do not possess the linguistic capabilities required to do so."

At this revelation, the auditorium was in an uproar. Dr Brown tried to restore order, saying loudly over the microphone, "Ladies and Gentlemen, please hear me, please listen and settle down, please, please." The noise gradually subsided. Daniel said, "OK, Ladies and Gentlemen, what we are now presented with is a situation which we have absolutely no control over. I know Zoe cannot lie. She has no motive for concocting a story like this, and she would never do so. What has happened, in effect, is that this race which, we shall refer to as the Greys, has released a biological weapon into our atmosphere in retaliation for mankind's brutal assault on their crewmen back in 1947. So, what do we do? In effect, there is nothing we can do. We cannot fight them, as we could never find them in space; even if we could find them, should we attack them for what was ultimately a reaction caused by our own arrogance and barbarism?"

Dr Brown then says, "We will now take a short break of around twenty minutes; there are refreshments: coffee, tea, and sandwiches in the hall opposite; please feel free to help yourselves. I would urge you all not to discuss what you have heard within the lecture during breaks, in the lecture, or the evenings. We are all bound by the Official Secrets Act. Any breach of which would incur severe penalties. Thank you for your attention! We shall resume in around twenty minutes."

Chapter Six

After around twenty minutes, Dr Brown made his way to the podium in the centre of the stage and began to speak, "Ladies and Gentlemen, we shall not dwell on the recent revelations. There is no point as there is nothing we can do about this situation. We just have to hope and pray that the offended race has reached the level of retribution, or a rate which they deem large enough to appease their anger. We shall now return to Zoe's diary entries:"

Dear, Diary, well, that was an eventful evening with Daniel and Lisa. I hope they weren't too upset with the information I had provided regarding the virus which their world is currently dealing with. I know we are meant to limit the amount of information we offer regarding other races, but I couldn't *not* tell them; they are very good friends of mine and Bens. That's me off to work now. I shall try and keep to the new regime Daniel has set out for me to not get involved in incidents or make myself obvious and noticeable to the rest of the population.

Good evening, Diary; well, that day didn't go well at all. I started work at 9 am as usual. I was at the checkout for a change today. I had been trained in many different jobs within the store by now. I didn't mind this job, but it was rather boring. I would rather be doing something more energetic. As the day progressed, the shop became very busy – a small queue had formed at the checkout. Totally out of the blue, a man came running down one of the aisles, went towards a woman who was standing in the queue, then grabbed her handbag, and ran out of the store.

The woman screamed "Stop, Thief," but the man had run off through the car park and up the street opposite. My initial instinct was to run after him and apprehend him, which I could have done quite easily with the speed I possess and the strength to subdue him. However, I remembered what Daniel had said about not getting involved or becoming too noticeable, so I did nothing but stand and look shocked. I felt awful because this was going against my natural moral instinct, which was to stop the man from doing wrong to another person.

The reasoning behind this is simple: if I am not being honest with myself, I am in effect, lying since my culture is based on rigorous morality and honesty; for me, to behave in this manner is the same as not saying something which I know I should, in effect, it's the same as lying and creates the sin of omission. I will speak to Daniel about this. It is a problem which has not occurred before, and Daniel has said on many occasions if anything causes us any trouble to please let him know. I will speak to Ben about this also; and see if he has encountered any similar situations; apparently, the transition to this new world is not going to be as easy as we initially thought.

Daniel then tells the audience, "Yes, well, Zoe did speak to me about this dilemma, and it is rather an unusual one. However, that will be enough for one day; thank you for your attendance and attention, Ladies, and Gentlemen. We shall resume tomorrow at 9 am sharp."

As Daniel drove the twenty-five miles to his home, he reflected on the events of the day.

Daniel thought, *so, the virus was, in effect, an alien attack on humanity for the past assault on their species; should we inform the powers that be about this? Then again, what can be done? As Zoe pointed out, even if we could find the species planet, should we then compound our initial assault on that species, or should we just accept that it was our own fault and there is, in fact, nothing we can do or should do in retaliation?*

When Dan got home, he went into the kitchen where Lisa was preparing their evening meal. Daniel went over and gave Lisa a big kiss. "How was your day, Honey?" Lisa asked.

"Yes, dear, it was very eventful, to say the least."

"Are you going to," Lisa interrupted, "go down to the garage until dinner is ready?"

"You know me so well, Dear," said Daniel laughing, "yes, I'll go and chill out for a little while. I have a bit of work to do in the garage; give me a shout when dinner's ready, Babes, yeah?"

Lisa said, "will do, Honey."

Daniel was working away in the garage on his new hobby, a kit car; he had decided to buy a kit and build a small car from scratch. This was something Daniel had always fancied doing, and it was worlds apart, something totally different from his usual life of teaching and lecturing. Dan was in the process of building the subframe when his phone rang in his office above the garage. He made his way up the staircase which was in the corner of the garage and answered it.

"Hey, Daniel, how are you, my friend?"

"Ben," Dan said, "yes, I'm good; cheers, Ben. I was going to give you a call this evening; you must be psychic," Dan said.

"I mean," Ben said laughing, "it's okay, Daniel. Zoe has told me about your conversations; how are you doing, Daniel?"

"I am very well, thanks, Ben! I was just going to ask, how you were finding your first few weeks here on earth?"

Ben said, "Yeah, good, Daniel, I've managed to get myself a job in a local garage, suits me great. I like mechanical stuff, and it keeps me fit at the same time."

"Excellent, Ben!" Daniel said. Have you managed to keep the diary I asked you to do? "Also, is it okay if I read it to the audience within the lecture I am currently presenting?"

Ben said, "Yes, of course, it is, Daniel. I have never kept a diary before, so I'm not sure how good it will be."

Daniel said, "It will be fine, Ben; it's only a record of your thoughts at the end of the day."

"Yes, Daniel, but some of my thoughts are, shall we say, rather different."

Dan said, "It will be fine, Ben; can you e-mail me a copy of what you have done up until now, so I can present it in my lecture, please?"

Ben said, "Yes, of course, I can, Daniel; just please don't expect too much from it."

Daniel laughed and said, "Don't worry; it will be fine."

The next morning, Dr Daniel Brown drove the twenty-five miles to the university where he was presenting this year's lecture. At precise three minutes to nine, he made his way onto the stage and to the podium in the centre, and at nine am precisely, Daniel began to speak.

"Good morning, Ladies and Gentlemen, and thank you for your attendance once again. This morning, we shall continue with a slightly different theme and explain a bit of what I mentioned earlier on the topic of 'self-healing.' Those of you who have read Descartes's theory on the mind-body split will follow this more easily, however, for those of you who have not, I will briefly outline the theory. Descartes's theory says that the mind and the body are two separate entities, however, the body can live indefinitely without the mind if it has artificial support. The mind, however, cannot live or operate as a mind without the body. While a brain can be preserved within a saline solution for a short period of time, it cannot function as a mind, while in that state requires a connected body to be a fully functional entity. This then dictates that if there is a split between mind and body which would appear to be the case if the body can exist albeit with artificial support, without the mind, where then does the joining of the two occur? This point of joining would inevitably be the soul or the essence of an individual."

There were small conversations throughout the auditorium, and mumbling, but nothing discernible, could be heard. Daniel continued, "The point is that when the mind is connected to the body, it has, in effect, control over that body, to the point where a person can slow down or speed up their own heartbeat. If then the mind has control over the internal bodily functions such as these, this would indicate that the mind has far greater control than we actually realise. If we could learn in the future to tap into our mind's capabilities, we could then have full control over everything which transpires within our own bodies."

"Think about it this way, your little toe, if and when you think about it, you can make it move. This is at the extremity of your physical body, so everything in between your mind and your little toe should, in effect, be accessible and controllable by your mind. The point I am making is that if we had total control over our bodies certain ailments would no longer constitute a problem. If we could get in touch with our inner self and say to our brain, okay, here it is, if this body dies, you can no longer exist, therefore, you need to repair it. There are obvious occasions where intervention is required e.g., dental work requires a dentist, or a bad cut requires stitches, whereas, a small cut on the skin will heal itself, all be it involuntary as far as we know, whether the brain has any actual control over this process is impossible to say at this moment in time. But if our mind has the capability to slow our heart rate down or speed it up, this indicates that we have far greater control over our bodies than we actually realise."

"Taking a small step back to the coronavirus, which Zoe covered earlier, there have been reports that some people have become ill after receiving the corona-virus vaccine. The theory is that these people have already, unknowingly, contracted the virus, and their bodies have already created antibodies, so the introduction of further antibodies is, in fact, having a detrimental effect on them. The reason for mentioning this is merely to point out how complex our bodies actually are. Also, the connection between the body triggers our built-in survival instinct, which we covered within the lecture last year. Therefore, if we could access and harness this built-in survival instinct, we would, in effect, be able to control much of what transpires within our own bodies."

"Where could this possibly begin, then? Meditation and concentration are the two keys to unlocking this treasure chest of self-healing powers." Daniel then says to the audience, "try this little exercise, pick something, anything, any item or even a spot on the wall. Okay, now see how long you can actually concentrate on that single item or spot on the wall before your mind wanders or having access to another thought or thoughts. If you are honest, it will not be a long period of time at all before your mind wanders. Once we have reached the point where we can meditate to the stage, where we have total concentration, then we can observe the possibility to utilise that concentration to greater use within our own bodies."

Dr Brown then says, "We shall now take a short break: tea, coffee, and sandwiches are available in the hall opposite; please feel free to help yourselves; we will resume in around twenty minutes, thank you!"

After around twenty minutes, the auditorium began to fill up again. Dr Brown made his way to the podium in the centre of the stage. Daniel began to speak:

Chapter Seven

last year, if you remember, we covered the correla"Within the lecture tion between God and the universe. It was explained that for the universe to be infinite, which we now accept, has to be the case, then God would also have to be infinite. As night follows day and day follows night, so is the case with the universe and God. It would, in effect, be impossible to have one without the other."

"Think on this for a moment: add one letter to the word God, and we have the word, Good; add one letter to the word evil, and we have the word, Devil. The words are so similar that I would suggest a linguistic curb has occurred over the ages, as in, evil was initially D-evil – the evil – and God was extended to become Good. Now, you may be thinking that this is all merely just a play on words and characters within the words. I offer it merely as an example of how words and perceptions can change over the ages. Also, with what Zoe has told us, we now have a different explanation for the existence of the Coronavirus. For whatever source or reason, at least, we are now able to battle the virus and hopefully keep it in check with the vaccines we have managed to develop."

"The reason for mentioning the words and the letters within the words, good and evil, God and Devil are only to highlight again the cyclical infinite motion of the universe and that which is contained therein. There could never be only good within the universe, nor could there be only evil. It is the combination that makes the universe a cyclical, infinite entity. In short, we require evil to recognise good, and we require good to recognise evil. It is, in effect, the same idea as finite beings only being recognised because there is an infinite being to comprehend them."

"In Zoe and Ben's home world, however, they have reached a point in their evolution where there is now an equilibrium, where there is no crime, yet they still retain their death penalty, should it be ever required, so they are not absolutely certain that crime will never occur again. Also, I had said at the beginning of this lecture that I would explain the reason for the secrecy behind the existence of Zoe and Ben in this world."

"During conversations with the two, it has become apparent that as well as possessing enhanced physical and mental abilities, compared to our own, their species are also, now, at a point in their evolution where they can control their own bodies' internal functions. Should anything go wrong, they can cure it with their minds. If this were to become common knowledge to our governments, they would, undoubtedly, pursue Zoe and Ben to learn their secrets. They would inevitably turn them into no more than lab rats, with never-ending experiments and tests to learn their secrets. Hence, their identities must forever remain a secret."

Daniel paused for a moment and adjusted some of the papers beside his laptop on the podium, "We shall now move on, and I would like to present to you some of Ben's diary entries. I must say, I have only had a brief look at the entries, but I will say that they are, at times, rather graphic, so let's move on. Here are some of the excerpts from Ben's diary:"

Ben's Diary

Hey, Book! How are you doing? Daniel has asked me to keep a little record of events since our arrival, so here we go. Nice house Daniel got me: a gym, a pool, lots of space, and modern appliances. One of the first things I had to do here was to get myself a job. I work out a lot, but I need some kind of achievement therapy as well. I had a stroll downtown to the local mall and looked at a few places around there. I found a small garage and went in.

The guy, who was working on one of the cars, said, "Hey, man! can I help you?"

I said, "Hope so, man. I'm looking for a job."

"Well, that depends; my name's Al, by the way, and this is my shop."

"Hi, cool! I'm Ben."

"Are you any good, Ben? I could use another pair of hands in the shop."

"Well, I've never had any complaints up until now, Al."

"Tell you what, we'll give you a trial for a week, see how it goes, that OK?"

"Yeah, that's great; cheers, man,"

"I'll tell you that Ford over there needs a new cylinder head gasket; fancy doing it today for me, it's only 11 am?"

I said, "Yeah, no worries, man." I had a quick google on my mobile phone to see what he was talking about; it turned out to be a piece of cake for me to do. It takes a fair amount of time to do the job, but I did it quicker than usual. I wasn't too quick, though. I didn't want to draw too much attention to myself. After a few hours, I said to Al, "There you are, all done, mate."

Al came over and started the car engine, then checked the temperature on the dashboard display; he said, "I'll be back in five minutes, just gonna take it for a test drive." He came back to the garage in five minutes and said, "Yeah, well, fuck the week's trial, you've got yourself a job, Ben. Hey, Joe! Jake! This is your new workmate, Ben."

The two mechanics shouted back, in turn, "Hey, Ben!" and I replied, "Hey, guys!"

Al said, "We'll see you in the morning, Ben; we start at eight and work until five; you get an hour's dinner break."

I said, "No worries, I'll see you in the morning, Man." It was a lovely afternoon, so I took a stroll home. I did my meditation, and then my workout, and a swim.

Then later, as I was relaxing by my pool, I heard a voice say, "Ahoy, shipmate, how are you doing?"

"Zoe, what a lovely surprise. How are you?"

"Yes, I am very well; thanks, Ben. I just needed to have a little chat, if that's okay?"

"Of course, it is, any time, Kid, you know that." I am only two years older than Zoe, but I've always been kind of like a big brother to her; even in our home world, she always looked up to me for advice and guidance. I said, "what can I do for you, Kiddo?"

Zoe said, "How are you finding life in this new world, Ben; do you foresee any problems with it?"

"No, not at all; why, have you come across a problem, Zoe?" I asked.

Zoe then told me about the guy who had run out of the store with the woman's bag and how she could have stopped him but remembering what Daniel had said about not being too noticeable did nothing. Zoe said she saw this as a kind of lying; the dishonesty involved was contrary to our moral beliefs. I told Zoe that, to be honest, I had done it automatically today when Al had asked me to do that job on the car in the garage. I knew I could have completed the work much quicker but didn't do so, as it would have drawn too much attention to myself.

Zoe said, "Do you not find it awkward to not be yourself?"

I said, "Zoe, listen, Kiddo; we are on a different planet, the same rules do not apply to us here, they have their own laws which we must abide by, but it's, as we said when we first arrived, we cannot enter their Olympic Games as we would win many medals."

"So, I shouldn't feel bad about not stopping shoplifters when I know I could easily do so?"

I told Zoe not to feel bad at all. That job is the responsibility of their security guard. Also, if she were to get hurt while tackling a shoplifter, Zoe would have no claim or come-back against her employer, as she should not have been doing that anyway. This whole new life is a learning curve for us; what applied to us morally in the home world doesn't always apply in this world, "Do you understand better now, Kid?"

Zoe said, "I do; it's just a bit more complicated than I initially realised. Anyway, that's great that you've managed to get yourself a job doing what you wanted, Ben."

"Yeah, Kid, I start tomorrow. I just did a little job for Al, the boss, today, as a kind of trial to see if I was any good."

I was drinking juice at this time when Zoe blurted out, "Have you had any unions yet, Ben?"

I wasn't expecting the question and choked a little bit on my juice while spitting it out and laughing at the same time. I said, "No, not yet, Kiddo, have you?"

"No, not yet, but there is a policeman who is going to call me soon to take me out for a drink or a meal, so, you never know," Zoe said laughing.

As I had said back, Zoe and I are like brother and sister; we have always been open and honest with each other about our relationships and the unions we have had.

Dr Brown then says to the audience, "If you all remember, a union is how these species refer to their sexual encounters or relationships. Zoe asking Ben if he has had a union yet is actually asking if he has had any sexual encounters or is in a relationship, and Ben is then asking her the same. We shall now return to Ben's diary entries."

Well, Book, Zoe stayed for a while, and we had a good laugh. I think she feels more at ease with the situation now and understands it better. She also told me about the encounters she had with the female essence from the next level. Also, how she had done some research and found out about the cover-ups that had occurred on occasion in this world. I told her it would be best to do what Daniel had said and not repeat the theories she had formulated. Due to our circumstances, it is best for us to keep a low profile.

Well, Book, I'm off to sleep now. I'm looking forward to starting my new job tomorrow; it'll be good getting to know my new workmates and getting some real work to do.

Good evening, Book, Well, that was an interesting day. I started work at 8 am in the morning, and it went really well; there was nothing that I couldn't do or cope with. Although I hadn't worked on these types of vehicles before, the basic theories of internal combustion engines are all the same, though me working with these machines with all the knowledge I possess is kind of like asking a brain surgeon to put a plaster on a cut finger. I can't grumble, though a job is a job at the end of the day. The truth be told, I will never get any job in this world that would align with my knowledge. Lunchtime was quite funny, Book, we had phoned out for burgers to be delivered, and after we had had lunch, we all sat down around a table in the back shop with a cup of coffee and started chatting.

The main topic of the day was the coronavirus. Jake had said, "What do you make of all this virus shit, Ben?"

I replied, "I dunno, a few theories are flying about, yeah?"

Jake said, "I'm not buying it, that it came from a bat in China, fuck that!"

Obviously, I knew already where it had originated but kept the conversation light. "Them, fuckin aliens, wasn't it?" I spoke.

"What?" Joe said.

"The aliens that crash-landed here years ago, you stole their technology and had done alien autopsies on them, so their mates came and attacked you with this virus."

Everybody, Al, Joe, and Jake were in fits of laughter. Al said, laughing, "fuck, that's the best theory I've heard yet, Ben; you're fucking crazy, man. You're gonna fit in here just fine."

I thought to myself, *well, my morality is intact, and I've been totally honest, this is a good day.* Joe had asked if I wanted to join him and Jake for a beer after work, and I had said, "Yeah, sure."

Al didn't join us; he was married and went straight home to his wife. I thought, *what a nice, caring guy.* We went to a bar not far from the garage.

After a few beers, Jake said, "So, Ben, how did you find your first day in the shop?"

I had to think for a second and then remembered that that was how they referred to the garage, the shop, as in the workshop. I said, "Yeah, I liked it. Nice place to work, Jake."

Joe said laughing, "Nah, it's the people you work with, man; are you coming to the cage fight on Saturday?"

I hadn't actually come across this term before so, I said, "Cage fight? I don't really watch much TV."

Joe said, "Cage fight, man, MMA mixed martial arts; you know, two guys or girls get in a cage and proceed to beat the shit out of one another."

"Ah, yes, of course, I have seen that before. Yeah, that'd be great."

"Cool," Jake said, "there's a crowd of us going; we'll meet in the bar here around 6:30 pm, have a few beers, then go to the venue."

"Great," I said, "I'll look forward to that."

Well, Book, this is going to be interesting, a fight. Absolutely, no one on this planet could beat me in a fight. I know, I am not fighting personally, but with the speed and strength I possess; this will be an interesting evening to see how these people perform. We stayed at the bar for a couple of hours and then said our goodbyes and went our separate ways; it was a good evening, Book. I got to know my new workmates a bit better, and it looks like I'll get to meet more people at the weekend. Sleep time now, and back to work tomorrow.

Dr Brown then says to the audience, "If you remember, these species are super fit compared to us; the speed and strength they possess, as well as superior mental abilities, and other attributes such as being able to hold their breath underwater for an extensive period of time and run at extraordinary speed, basically makes them superhuman compared to ourselves. If you notice, though, that Ben has dealt with the subject of the coronavirus without compromising his honesty or moral ethic, whereas, Zoe felt rather compromised to divulge the truth about the virus to Lisa and me. I did phone Zoe recently to ask how she was coping with her new regime of keeping a low profile, and I was quite surprised at what she said."

When I called, I said, "Hi, Zoe! How's it going at the shop?"

"Hi, Daniel, yes, it is going very well, thank you!"

"Are you managing to keep a low profile, as we talked about?"

"Yes, Daniel, it turns out to be no problem at all; also, I can still retain my honesty and morality."

Now, I was intrigued, "How do you manage that?"? I asked.

Zoe said, "It's actually turned out to be quite simple, Daniel, for example, I was walking down one of the aisles today, and I saw a shoplifter putting items into a bag." I said, "Yes, on you go, help yourself; hearing, this he just dropped the bag he had in his hand and ran out of the store."

I couldn't stop laughing. "Well done, you, Zoe!" I spoke.

Zoe said, "On another occasion, I saw a girl put a screwdriver into her coat and down her jeans." Zoe had said to her, "Oh, dear, be careful and don't hurt yourself with that."

The girl said, "Sorry, I was going to pay for it at the check-out. I'll just put it back."

"OK, no problem," I said, "so, you see, Daniel, it's not difficult to retain my honesty and morality and still help my employer to save money by not having items stolen."

"Excellent, Zoe! So long as you keep a low profile. I am only concerned for your welfare."

Zoe said, "Yes, Daniel, I know you are, thank you!"

Dr Brown then says to the audience, "What we can see emerging, then is a pattern, whereby, both Zoe and Ben, are finding ways to get around their rigorous honesty and morality without actually having to lie and or drawing too much attention to themselves."

Dr Brown continues, "We will now take a short break; refreshments are available in the hall opposite, we will resume in around twenty minutes, thank you!"

The audience applauded for a short period of time, then the applause subsided, and the patrons started to make their way to the hall opposite.

After around twenty minutes, the auditorium started to fill up again. Dr Daniel Brown made his way to the podium located in the centre of the stage and began to speak, "Thank you, Ladies and Gentlemen! We shall now return to the entries from Ben's diary:

Hey, Book, I'm back. Sunday morning was a beautiful morning, and I've had a great workout today, turns out, I had

had a little workout last night, as well. I met the guys in the bar around 6:30 as arranged. There were around ten guys in our group. Jake and Joe introduced me to all the guys in turn, and we all had a few beers. When it was time to make our way to the venue for the cage fights, we all started to walk through the centre of town; it was quite busy as it was Saturday night, and there were lots of clubs and bars open and lots of people out and about. As we joined the queue, which was moving quite quickly into the building, I noticed that there was a mixture of males and females waiting to go into the venue.

Joe said, "Have you been to a cage fight before, Ben?"

"No, Joe, never before," I said.

"Just watch out for the ass-holes; you always get a few," Joe said, "the testosterone gets flowing when they watch the fights, and before you know it, some of them start thinking they're Bruce Lee and want to have a go themselves.

I said, "I'll keep an eye open for those."

There was no drinking alcohol allowed within the venue, although most of the men had already had quite a few beers before they got there. When it was time for the first fight, everyone started cheering the fighters as they entered the cage. After the introductions and instructions from the referee as to what was and what was not allowed within the fight, they faced each other from either side of the arena, then the bell rang. The fight was over in seconds – there was no biting, gouging, or pulling hair allowed, but everything else was acceptable.

The objective was to punch and kick your opponent until he could no longer defend himself; the other option was to subdue your opponent in a hold-down whereby he couldn't move nor retaliate. On this occasion, one man just ran across the ring and knocked his opponent to the floor with a flying kick, then proceeded to level punches after punches to his head. The referee only allowed this to continue for a few seconds then intervened, obviously for the fighters' safety; as I said, the fight was over in seconds.

Jake said, "Fuck me, did you see that?"

I said, "Yes, fuck me, very impressive!"

Jake looked a bit funny, and I wondered if I had said something wrong, but he didn't say anything. The next three fights were of varying durations; one of them was a female contest. I thought to myself, *if Zoe were here, she could show you both a thing or two,* but then again, we wouldn't be able to participate in this sport as our knowledge and skills are far too great.

Then, they announced that it was time for an interval; soft drinks and snacks were available at a kiosk. Joe said, "Fancy a juice, Ben?"

"Yeah, sure, it's hot in here, and I am quite thirsty."

As we made our way to the kiosk, this guy barged into my shoulder. I looked at him, expecting an apology, then realised he had done it on purpose. Joe saw it and said, "What the fuck are you doing, man?" The man put his hand out to grab Joe. I grabbed the man's wrist; we have extensive knowledge of the human body, exactly where all the pressure points are, and how to render an individual helpless in seconds.

The man was on his knees, squealing in pain in a second, "Let me go, let me go, I'm sorry!" he said.

I let him go and said, "Don't fuck with me."

The guy got up and walked away. Joe said, "Well, looks like you can handle yourself, Ben."

I said, "Yeah, I've done a little bit of martial arts before." That wasn't a lie as such, so I was still within my moral boundaries. I just didn't go into detail as to how much martial arts I actually knew. We got our juice and returned to where we were standing.

Joe said to Jake and Al, "You should see this guy handle himself; he should be in the cage."

Al said, "Why? What happened?"

Joe said, "Ah, just one of the usual ass-holes you get at these things; all's good."

We watched the rest of the bouts; some of the techniques were better than others, and I thought to myself, *to me, this would be a waste of time, but then again, it's a different world and a different race, so I shouldn't be too critical.* As we got out of the venue, I saw the guy that I had grabbed; he saw me and pointed me out to his mates, "That's the one who grabbed my wrist."

One of his mates said, "Really, he's a big guy; let's see how big?"

I didn't want the guys getting involved; they may have gotten hurt, so I said, "You guys, go on down the road. I'll catch you up after I've dealt with this."

Jake said, "There's four of them; will you be, okay?"

Joe said laughing, "I've seen what he can do; he'll be okay, let's go."

The guys started walking down the street as the guy I had grabbed; and his mates came over, "What's wrong with your mates; they not helping you?"

I said, "Look, guys, I don't want any trouble, and I have no wish to hurt you, so let's just leave it."

One guy said, "Get him."

I ran down a nearby ally where no one would see what would be going on. They chased me. I leapt around twenty feet in the air; the four guys just looked up in amazement, and as I came down, a couple of kicks and two back fists, and it was all over in seconds. All four were unconscious and lying on the ground. I ran down the road where the guys had gone and shouted, "Wait up, You Lot."

Jake said, "Hey, man, you, okay? That was quick."

"Yeah, I'm fine. I guess they didn't learn anything from the fights tonight," I said laughing, "let's get a beer, yeah?" The guys were laughing; we made our way back to the bar and had a few beers; it had been a good night, and I got a little work out into the bargain.

When we got to the bar, it was quite different from earlier, the music was very loud, and there were lots of females on the dance floor. I said to Joe, "Well, this is different from earlier."

Joe said, "Yeah, they change it into a disco bar on Saturday nights; plenty talent, eh?"

I smiled and said, "Yeah, not bad at all." I thought to myself, *it's been a few years since I had a union, I could really do with one.* I guess Zoe had planted that seed earlier when she mentioned her new acquaintance, Zak. As we found a table and got a few beers in, I caught a glimpse of a girl looking at me. I looked back and smiled, "I'll be back shortly, Boys," I said.

"Fuck, you don't waste any time, do you, Ben?" Joe said.

I went over to the woman and said, "Hi, how are you doing? My name's Ben."

"Hi, nice to meet you, Ben. My name's Jo."

"Oh, that's a coincidence, one of my mates is also called Joe," I said. "But, I've got to say he's not nearly as pretty as you," I said, laughing.

Jo said, "Well, who's the sweet talker, then?" We chatted for a while, and Jo told me she worked at a hairdresser's in the mall in town. I told her I was a mechanic, which worked out great as she asked me to come to her house the next day to take a look at her car as it wasn't working properly, "No power when you accelerate," she said. And she said that she would cook Sunday dinner for both of us, while I had a look at her car.

We spent the rest of the night together. I took her over and introduced her to the guys at one point. Al said, "Ah, she's lovely, Ben."

We left together and got a cab; I dropped her off first, and she invited me in for a drink. We chatted for a while as she told me about her life and her past, how she had made a few mistakes and taken up the wrong guys. I said that the past was irrelevant and that it was 'now' and the 'future' that mattered.

After we had arranged a time for me to come over the next day, I called a cab; we said our good-nights, and I made my way home. After she'd told me about her previous relationships, I realised that she had been quite hurt in the past. She was very pretty, but definitely not the type of girl to enter into a one-night union. I am not ready for any long-term relationship and not sure if I ever will be, so for the moment, it was just nice to have some female company other than Zoe or Lisa. Sleep for me now, Book.

Dr Brown then says to the audience, "As you can see from the diary entries, both Ben and Zoe are dealing with their new lives very differently, which you would obviously expect them, being a man and a woman respectively. As well as possessing superior physical skills and abilities, their mental abilities are also far superior to our own. They are both well aware of the concept of cause and effect within the universe, and also about the same concept that applies to personal relationships. They are both extremely caring individuals. Although Zoe had mentioned on the night out with Lisa that she had had a few one-night unions in the past, she was referring to her life around twenty years before. Zoe is now forty-five years old but looks around twenty-five of our earth years age, and Ben is forty-seven but looks around twenty-seven. The reason for mentioning this is to point out what I had already discussed with them both; if they were to enter into relationships in this world, they would probably have to accept a partner that was around twenty years younger than themselves."

"The other problem being that their superior fitness and athletic abilities mean that they may have to tone down their own libido to match that of any prospective partner," Daniel says to the audience laughing, "it would be a hell of a way to go to the next level, but Zoe and Ben would probably still be liable for some kind of assault or murder charge."

The audience was all laughing and applauding. Daniel waited a few moments to allow the noise to subside, then continued, "I did ponder for some time on whether to read out the next few diary entries from both Zoe and Ben, but as they are rather graphic and explicit, to say the least, and since this is not a sex education lesson, I am not going into the erotic details of the next few diary entries. What I will tell you is that Zoe did have a dinner date with her policeman acquaintance,

Zak, and to cut a long story short, she did initiate a union that evening. Zoe is very beautiful, and Zak had no hesitation when she suggested taking their relationship further. The problem, as I pointed out earlier, is the difference in stamina between the two races. Immediately after their encounter, which Zoe stated, 'Did not last very long at all,'" she instantly terminated the relationship. Zak asked Zoe what was wrong. Zoe did not lie to him; she just said, "I'm sorry, but you just know when something is not quite right, and there is no point in pursuing it further, however, we can still remain, friends, if you wish, but there will be no further unions."

Zak said, "Sure, whatever you want."

When Ben went to Jo's house for Sunday lunch and to fix her car, Jo too initiated an encounter later that evening. Ben entered into his diary that he was quite surprised as he didn't think Jo would want to have a sexual relationship quite so soon, however, as he had said earlier, Ben had not had a union for many years and was quite happy to pursue what he thought was a one-night union. Unlike Zoe, however, Jo was, shall we say, more than satisfied with Ben's performance, and Jo wanted to make their relationship more permanent. This was the difficult part for Ben, as much as he enjoyed Jo's company and their union; he was not ready to commit to a long-term relationship. Like Zoe, he did not lie; he merely told Jo that he wasn't ready to commit to a long-term relationship; the best he could offer her at this time was a close friendship. Jo said, "that's okay, let's just take it as it comes, yeah?"

Dr Brown then addresses the audience, "So, you can see that there is a pattern developing for the two aliens: Ben is adapting well to his new environment, where Zoe is finding it quite difficult to come to terms with her new life on earth. Mainly because of her superior fitness and stamina, she is, in effect, far more fit and powerful than the males of our species. This poses various problems for Zoe, for as much as we promote sexual equality within our society, in reality, most of the time, the females of our species shall always be the weaker sex when it comes to strength and stamina."

"This poses another problem for Zoe as she cannot lie, so to pretend to be less strong or fit than she actually is to fit into the earth female role would, in effect, be a lie she would not be true to herself. Ultimately, she could not do this. Ben, on the other hand, can live here on earth quite happily and be himself without changing anything at all."

Daniel says to the audience, "So, you can see that it is not so simple to move to another planet where there are certain differences in strength and stamina between two different species. That will be all for today; we shall resume tomorrow at 9 am sharp; thank you for your attendance and your attention!"

The audience stood up and applauded as Dr Brown left the stage. Daniel smiled and made several gestures of acknowledgement.

As Dr Daniel Brown drove home, he reflected on the events of the day and the diary entries he had presented; he wondered if there was any way he could help Zoe to come to terms any better with her new life here. When Daniel arrived home, he went into the kitchen and over to Lisa, who was preparing their evening meal in the kitchen; he gave her a big kiss and said, "Good evening, Honey!"

Lisa replied, "Hi, Babes, how did it go today?"

"Yes, I think it went quite well; there were no complaints, anyway," Dan said, laughing.

"Garage?" Lisa said.

Dan replied, laughing, "Oh, well, okay. I'll go down for a little while until dinner's ready, baby."

As Daniel made his way through their large garden, his mobile rang. "Hi, Daniel, how are you doing?"

"Hi, Ben, yes, I'm fine, thanks, and how are you?"

Ben replied, "yeah, I'm good; cheers, Daniel, how did they like my book?"

Ben had mastered much of our slang already, like cheers, and yeah, man. Dan said, "Yes, it was very well-presented, Ben. I did leave out the graphic encounter of your union with Jo."

Ben said, "I didn't know how explicit you wanted the entries to be, Dan, so I just put it in, the way it was."

Daniel said, "No, it was fine, Ben, I just didn't see the point in relaying all of what is, in effect, your personal sex life to the audience. I did point out that it was not a sex education lesson they were attending."

Ben said, "Okay, cool, Daniel, whatever you think."

Dan said, laughing, "I must admit to being rather jealous at some points within those particular entries, Ben."

"Oh, sorry, man, well, yeah, it was a good night, although it was a bit less energetic than usual," said Ben.

Dan said with a surprised look, "Less energetic, oh okay; are you still seeing Jo?"

"Hell, yeah," said Ben, "we are the best of buddies; she's great."

Dan said, "I was going to talk to you about Zoe, Ben. Is there anything we can do to make her transition any easier?"

Ben said, "Yeah, she wasn't best pleased with that Zak's performance."

Dan said, "Oh, I didn't know that Ben, I haven't read that part of her diary yet. I meant about her having to change her regime while working at the shop, like not tackling shoplifters."

Ben said, "Yeah, I told her about that that she could get into trouble as that was the security guard's job," Ben said laughing, "Sorry, Daniel, I thought you were referring to Zoe's union with Zak."

Dan said, "Zoe hasn't said anything to me about this; is she okay?"

"Yeah, she's fine; she's just not too impressed with the males of your species at the moment," Ben said, laughing.

"Oh," said Daniel, "I take it that her union with Zak wasn't as successful as yours was with Jo?"

Ben said, "Hell, no, she wasn't happy at all. To help you understand, Daniel, Zoe and I are like brother and sister, although, we're not related, she tells me everything," Ben continued, "don't worry about Zoe, Daniel, she will meditate and find any answers she needs within her meditations this is how we are taught how to deal with any problems; we meditate on the lessons taught by the teacher and find the answers we need from these."

Daniel said, "Okay, Ben, that's good; I just don't want her to feel alienated, pardon the pun."

Both Ben and Daniel started laughing, then Daniel said, "I know some of your cultures and just don't want Zoe to get so down that she takes the opt-out option."

Ben said, "She would tell me first if she was considering that option, Daniel; we do have the opt-out pill with us; we have several actually, just in case we needed to help someone with an assisted opt-out."

Dan was totally shocked by this revelation. He said to Ben, "Surely, you can't exercise that option in this world?"

Ben said, "We are still in charge of our own, lives Daniel; if we could find no answer within the meditations or the teachings that were acceptable to us, we still retain the option of the voluntary opt-out."

Daniel said, "Yes, Ben, but what you said about helping someone, that would be, in effect, an assisted suicide, which is totally illegal in this country."

"You can put your phone down now, Daniel."

Daniel turned around, and Ben was standing in the doorway of the garage, "I thought since we were having such a long conversation, I'd come and see you face-to-face, Daniel."

"Lovely surprise, Ben, it's always good to see you, my friend," said Daniel.

"I drove over in a car I brought home from the shop. I'm going to work on it tonight. I didn't get that job finished today," said Ben.

"Is it a big job?" Asked Daniel.

"No, it's only a bit of body touch-up and paint. I'll do it later," continued Ben. "I know some of your laws, Daniel, I know now that would be classed as an assisted suicide, we didn't know all your laws before we came, and hence, we brought the extra pills; obviously, now, we couldn't use them to help others opt-out."

Daniel breathed a sigh of relief, "I'm glad we got that sorted out, Ben."

"There are lots of contradictions within your society, Daniel, it's said, within your book of teachings, that you should not worship craven images, yet billions of your population still worship an instrument of torture and eventual death, this wooden cross. Do you think your teacher would have desired this, Daniel?"

Daniel said, "Well, when you put it like that, no, I don't imagine that he would, although the people are only remembering how he died."

Ben said, "Daniel, you know from your crew's report that was sent back, that our teacher lived a long and exceptional life then chose to opt-out himself, we remember his teachings, not the way he died," Ben continued, "the people of your world claim to be so religious, yet their morality is severely lacking."

Daniel laughed and said, "Ben, my friend, I totally understand what you are saying, but we have an old saying in this world: when you are in the boozer, never discuss politics or religion as they are way too subjective, and as in there are no right or wrong answers," Daniel then said, "would you like a cold beer, Ben?"

"Yeah, man, that'd be great; cheers."

"Hey guys, have you got one for us?"

Daniel and Ben looked towards the door of the garage. It was Zoe and Lisa. Lisa said, "I have put dinner on hold for just now, Honey. Ben and Zoe, would you like to join us for dinner?"

Zoe said, "I'd like that," and Ben said the same.

Lisa said, "It's a lovely evening; what say we have a few drinks on the patio first, then have dinner?"

"That's a great idea, Honey, we'll do that. How did you get here, Zoe?" asked Daniel.

Zoe said, "I called Lisa to ask if I could pop over for a chat, then took a cab. Daniel, hope you don't mind?"

Daniel said, "Not at all, and neither of you needs an invitation. It's always a pleasure to see you both."

Ben scrapped the idea of working on the car tonight. He was enjoying the beers and the company. "I'll just get a cab home later," Ben said, "I can't drive with a few beers in me."

Zoe said, "I'll share the cab with you when we go, Ben."

"Never discuss politics or religion, Zoe," Ben said, "it's not allowed here as it is too subjective."

Zoe said laughing, "Okay, how many beers have you had, Ben."

Daniel interrupted, laughing, "Zoe, that was part of a conversation we were having earlier; it's a kind of rule of thumb, when you're drinking don't discuss these topics as it always leads to arguments."

Ben then looked at his thumb and said, "I didn't know you had rules."

Everyone was laughing now; neither Zoe nor Ben had heard that expression before. Daniel explained that initially, it was an ancient means of measurement but was now, just a saying when referring to a hypothetical measurement. The four sat on the patio for a couple of hours, then had a lovely dinner. Zoe and Ben said their good-nights and took a cab home.

The next morning, as Dr Daniel Brown drove the twenty-five miles to the university and made his way to the auditorium, he reflected on what a great night he and Lisa had shared with Ben and Zoe. Dan had decided that there was no point in contacting the authorities regarding Zoe's revelations surrounding the origins of the Coronavirus. the number of positive infections seemed to be falling now, whether that was due to the introduction of the vaccines, or the fact that the original perpetrators had decided not to release any further strains of the virus, he did not know.

Also, how could Daniel possibly explain where he had squired the information regarding the origin of the virus. When Dr Brown made his way to the podium in the centre of the stage at three minutes to nine, the audience was already seated. At 9 am precisely, Dr Daniel Brown began to speak.

Chapter Eight

"Good morning, Ladies and Gentlemen, and thank you for attending once again; today, we shall be looking at further excerpts from both Ben and Zoe's diaries. Before we do that, though, I would ask you to cast your minds back to the lecture last year. If you remember, we touched on the subject of the three pyramids on the Giza plateau in Egypt, how ten thousand five hundred years ago, they lined up exactly with the three stars within the star constellation we now know as Orion. During my long conversations with Zoe and Ben, it became apparent that this occurrence was not new to them. In their home world, they too have three pyramids which, ten thousand five hundred years ago, also lined up exactly with the three stars within one of the constellations in their own solar system."

"They know this to be the case from their own computer projections, they do not know, however, who built the pyramids originally, or what their actual purpose was, they just know that they have been there for many thousands of years."

"This is just some food for thought to reiterate how much we do not actually know about the universe, but it is very interesting," Daniel continued, "we shall now proceed with some excerpts from Zoe's diary:"

Dear Diary, that was a great night with Daniel and Lisa last night, with Ben there as well; we had a lovely chat and lots of laughs in the garden, then a lovely meal which Lisa had made: I love chicken. Unfortunately, I had to terminate my relationship with Zak. It wasn't really a relationship, as such, since we were only together for one night. As I said to him, you just know when something is not going to work, he is a very nice man but rather demure compared to some of the unions I have had in the past. He is looking to settle down and get married, then start a family. I, on the other hand, am not. I was only looking for a short or possibly frequent union; I got the short bit correct anyway. He looked quite masculine and fit, but as they say, looks can be deceptive; he had no stamina at all and very limited experience with the opposite sex. I was the one who initiated the union, but our encounter didn't last long at all; it was more of a disappointment than a union, hence, the prompt termination. I would still speak to him if I bumped into him, but I wouldn't go for a meal or drink with him again, too slow and boring for me, I'm afraid, but as one of my new friends says, hey ho, onwards and upwards.

Daniel says to the audience, "So, you see that Zoe has had her first sexual encounter with an earth male, which hasn't turned out very well for her. However, Zoe doesn't seem too bothered, as I said before, both Zoe and Ben have been rigorously checked and re-checked in their home world for their ability to deal with any situation. Although I have had to speak to Zoe regarding becoming too noticeable to the wider population, she is and has adapted well to her new environment."

"Ben too has adapted well, albeit, in a different way from Zoe; he now has friends, workmates, a female acquaintance with whom he can, apparently, form a union on occasion. They are both just taking life as it comes and dealing with the various day-to-day new experiences which arise if there was anything they were not quite sure of, or how to best deal with, they know they can contact me or Lisa for advice anytime." Dr Brown continues, "I would now like to present to you an interesting excerpt from Ben's diary:

Hey, Book, how are you doing? Daniel and I had a very interesting conversation last night. I took a ride over to Daniel and Lisa's house on my new motorcycle; they call it a Harley, and it is very smooth and fast, a perfect way for me to get around. I got to Daniel's around 7:30 pm. He and Lisa were just about to have dinner, and Daniel was back in the garage working on his kit car. I said, "Hey, Daniel, how's it going?"

"Ah! Just the man I needed. You've appeared just at the right time, Ben. I could really do with help on this bit," Daniel had reached a tricky bit whilst constructing the sub-frame of his little car, so I was glad to be able to help.

While we were working away, I said to Daniel, "Daniel, have you ever wondered about all of this?"

Dan said, "What do you mean, Ben?"

"I mean everything, the universe, our different planets, the next level, everything, have you ever doubted any of it?"

Daniel then said, "I'll tell you a little story, Ben. I've never told anyone this before. A few years ago, one of Lisa's close friends had lost one of their family members; they passed away very suddenly. I had never met them and did not know them at all. When Lisa told me, she was a bit upset as she had known the family for many years; what happened next was astonishing. The next morning, I was lying in my bed, about to get up. I felt this presence in the bedroom, right at the side of me like it was looking down on me. It was very surreal as I knew something was there but didn't know what. I remember thinking this can't be the person Lisa knew that had passed away recently as I didn't know them, they wouldn't come to see me from the next level."

"Well, after a few moments, the presence left the room, and I got up and got ready for work. A couple of days later, we attended the funeral of Lisa's friend's family member then I went back to work within the university where I was working at that time."

"Three days later, Lisa phoned me at work," she said, "I don't know how to tell you this, Honey, a very good friend of mine whom I had known for twenty years had passed away very suddenly and traumatically, they had taken their own life, or opted-out, as you call it, Ben. I never thought he was capable of that; his funeral was to take place within the next half an hour, so obviously, I couldn't attend. I would not be able to get there in time.

"Then, I remembered the presence in the room a few days before, it was my friend who had come to say goodbye, but he had also come to let me know that the next level actually did exist. He and I had had many extended conversations regarding life, psychology, philosophy, and the afterlife; he had come to let me know that there was, in fact, the next level. So, you see. Ben, since then, I have never doubted the existence of the next level; the experience of that presence will stay with me forever. That was why I never doubted Zoe for one minute, not that I would, anyway, when she told us of her encounters with the female essence."

"Wow, cool, Daniel!" Ben continued, "I know we were not meant to discuss religion, Daniel, but I do have a couple of questions if you don't mind?"

Daniel said, "Okay, Ben, fire away."

Ben said, "When we arrived here last year, we told you that if you decipher our teacher's reference to the universe and his father's house. Do you remember, in my father's house, there are many mansions, meaning the numerous planets in the universe which can propagate and support life?"

Daniel said, "Yes, Ben, I remember the correlation between God and the universe."

Ben said, "Yes, Daniel, exactly, I have also been doing a bit more research. It appears that within your Holy Book, your citizens have drawn certain assumptions. In your book, your teacher says, 'are you surprised you must be reborn to know my father's kingdom,'" Ben continued, "now you guys have assumed that having someone throw water over yourselves constitutes rebirth, when what the reference actually means is leaving this existence and moving to the next level where your essence exists infinitely."

Daniel said, "I can understand that line of thinking, Ben, but the throwing of the water is a symbolic gesture, the same as our holy communion. When we eat a piece of bread and drink some wine, we know it's not really the body and the blood; it is merely a symbolic gesture. It is easy to see how the interpretations could be misunderstood, Ben."

"As I said before, everyone's thoughts and perceptions on religion are different; this is why it's better not being discussed, everyone is entitled to their own interpretation and to adopt what suits them best."

Ben said, "Okay, Daniel, no worries, let's crack on with your car and get this sub-frame built, yeah?"

Daniel then says to the audience, "I fully understand what Ben is saying, as I said, it is up to the individual which translation they adopt and decide to believe in from any text to understand this better we can always refer back to the subjective and objective views within an ontology. On a much lighter note, Lisa and I held a barbecue a couple of weeks ago, some of you were there; we had also invited Zoe and her new friends and workmates, and Ben and his new workmates and friends. I also invited some acquaintances I had encountered while I was a psychological consultant for the sex re-assignment department during a recent study placement. These particular invitations were mainly for Zoe and Ben's benefit, as they had both indicated that one of the reasons, they wished to remain on earth, was due to the numerous deviations and the physical freedom that exists in our world. We all had to have our stories straight as to where Zoe and Ben had come from originally, and how they have ended up living in this part of the country. We shall now look at one of Ben's diary entries:"

Hey, Book, how are you doing? I am so looking forward to Daniel and Lisa's barbecue on the weekend. *That* John is going to be there too. I hope he behaves this time and Zoe doesn't have to kick him into the pool. I am also looking forward to Daniel and Lisa meeting Jo for the first time; she is such a lovely lady; we get on really well. I'm sure Daniel and Lisa will like her too. Al and his wife, Jake, and Joe from my work are also invited, as well as a few guys from the bar. I'll make sure they all behave. Some of Daniel's friends from his current lecture are coming also, and some of Lisa's and Zoe's girlfriends so, it's going to be quite a diverse crowd; it should be good fun.

There was a bit of drama in the shop today. Joe was working on a Nissan and he had it jacked up at one side; there were only two ramps, and Jake and I were using them. What happened next was an absolute fluke; a few kids were passing the garage, it was lunchtime, and they had come to the shops from a local college to get some snacks. One of the kids had a basketball; he was bouncing it on the ground and onto the wall as he went along. It all happened very quickly. The kid had bounced the ball on the wall opposite the garage and failed to catch it on its return. The ball bounced into the workshop; the large door was always open fully as the weather was so nice. The ball hit the jack handle underneath the Nissan, which Joe was working on. Joe let out an almighty yell; the wheel of the truck had landed on his foot. I jumped right over and lifted the truck enough for Joe to get his foot out from under the wheel.

"Cheers, man," Joe said, "but how the fuck did you manage to lift that?"

I said, "I don't know, man, must've been all that weight-lifting training I used to do. What I lifted, must have weighed around a ton, but I never thought at the time, how it would look, me being able to lift that amount of weight. Thankfully, no one paid too much attention regarding me lifting the truck; they were all just glad Joe wasn't injured seriously. Jake threw the ball back to the kid, who shouted to say he was sorry and that it was an accident, which we knew already. At lunchtime, we sat in the back shop and had coffee and burgers,

"How's your foot, Joe?" asked Al.

"Yeah, it's okay, Man. I'm just glad Ben ain't a weakling; cheers again, Ben," Joe said.

"No worries, man," I said. I changed the subject quickly, "Hey guys, did you see the news last night; they have landed a spaceship on Mars?"

Jake said, "Yeah, Man, they're still looking for fuckin aliens; they should stop wasting all that money and just accept that aliens don't exist."

I said, "So, do you not think there is life in other worlds then, Jake."

Jake said, "No way, Man, little green men, or big hairy ant things, I'm not buying any of it."

So, by now, I'd realised that I'd picked the wrong subject to change to.

Joe said, "Hey, Man, I'm looking forward to your friends' barbecue on Sunday. That's so nice of them to invite all of us."

I said, "They're a great couple, very good friends of mine. I'm sure it will be a great day."

Dr Brown then says to the audience, "Well, yes, it was a great day, however, I won't say too much as it is pretty well covered in the diary entries by Ben and Zoe. What I will say is that the invitation list was mainly to accommodate Ben and Zoe, welcoming them to their new world. We shall now look at one of Zoe's diary entries:"

Dear Diary, this was a busy day at work. Mike asked me to be on the till for the first few hours, then I was to unpack a delivery we had just received. I like it when it's busy; the day seems to go much faster, not that I want the day to go faster, I just don't like standing about doing nothing. I was speaking to Lucy today and asked her if she would like to attend Daniel and Lisa's barbecue on Sunday, "Hey, girl…"

"Yeah, sure! Are you asking me on a date, Honey," Lucy said, laughing.

"No, Lucy, just as a friend. Mike and his wife are coming as well. Daniel and Lisa are very good friends of mine, and they wondered if I would like to introduce them to my new friends and colleagues."

Lucy said, "Is it okay if I bring a friend along with me too?"

"Yes, of course, it is. Do you have a new girlfriend?"

Lucy said, laughing, "She's not my girlfriend yet, but I'm working on it if you know what I mean."

I just smiled and said, "Okay, that's great. I'll give you the address for the barbecue later today."

"Okay, Honey, thanks for that," Lucy said.

Dear Diary, it was a wonderful day at Daniel and Lisa's barbecue, actually very eventful. I had picked Ben up on the way, and we arrived at around 11 am; we took a cab as we knew we would be partaking in a little alcohol throughout the day. We weren't the first to arrive. Kate and a few of Lisa's friends were there already. Their children were also playing with Daniel and Lisa's kids, the sun was shining, and it was a beautiful day for a barbecue. John arrived, sober as a judge; he came over and said, "Hello, Zoe, very nice to see you again."

I replied, "Hi, John, nice to see you sober." Al and his wife arrived from Ben's work. Ben introduced me; they were both very nice. Then, Jake and Joe arrived. Al shouted over, "Hey guys,"

"Hey, Joe, the wife not coming?"

Joe replied, "Working, be here later." I thought to myself, *Well, no luck there.*

"He's married, Ben," I said.

Ben said, "Apparently so, I've never heard him mention a wife, but I have only worked there for a short while."

"That's a pity; he's a good-looking guy," I said.

Ben said, "Down, Zoe," laughing.

Jake was a big man, rough-looking with a big shaggy beard, not what I would consider being a good-looking guy, or so I thought. The garden was starting to fill up, lots of people were arriving now. Daniel had hooked up a microphone and speaker to avoid shouting. When everyone was gathered, there weren't many people left to appear, Daniel made an announcement:

"Everyone, everyone, can I have your attention for a moment, please. Lisa and I would like to welcome you all to our humble home and hope you all enjoy the events of the day; there is plenty of alcohol and soft drinks situated in various stands around the garden; and within the house, so please just help yourselves. John, remember what I told you earlier," Daniel said, laughing.

John put his head in one hand and the other in the air, then laughed loudly, "Okay, Daniel, no worries," he said.

I was loving this. I really enjoy meeting new people and seeing different styles of life. I looked over the garden and saw Ben speaking to his workmate, Jake. I went over and said, "Hi, Ben, aren't you going to introduce me to your big burly friend?"

Ben laughed and said, "Jake, this is a very good friend of mine, Zoe, my little sis from another life."

"Hi, Zoe, pleased to meet you. Ben talks about you all the time."

"Do you, Ben?" I said.

Jake butted in and said, "Actually, he's never mentioned you before, and you are absolutely beautiful, so I wonder why he hasn't."

"Oh, you, flatterer," I said, "thank you very much!"

Jake then said, "Well, I guess that's as far as we are going to go, you won't want anything to do with an ugly mug like me."

As I walked away, I said, "Jake, My Darling, beauty is in the eye of the beholder; never say never."

Ben told me a little later that Jake had said to him that if he could wake up to me saying "my darling" every morning, his life would be complete. I think Jake really likes me.

Dr Brown then addresses the audience, "I will intervene for a moment here to point out that, although Zoe is very beautiful, she is not at all narcissistic. Also, Zoe is not concerned with how a prospective partner looks, although she can judge who is a good-looking man, this is not the top priority for Zoe to pursue a relationship. She is more concerned with other qualities, such as honesty, loyalty, trustworthiness, and caring nature. We shall now take a look at one of the excerpts from Ben's diary:

Hey Book, how are you doing? Well, that was a blast at Daniel and Lisa's barbecue, with quite a few unexpected surprises, to say the least. Zoe picked me up in a cab on the way to Daniel and Lisa's; we arrived around 11 am. Daniel and Lisa have a beautiful big house and garden, with a large pool and a double garage. Al and his wife, Jenny, arrived soon after us. We all got a drink and had a stroll on the grounds. John arrived shortly after, sober as a judge.

Zoe said, "That's Lucy and her friend coming in now, Ben."

I said, "Cool, come on and introduce me."

We went over to Lucy and her friend, Zoe said, "Hi, Lucy, this is my friend, Ben."

Lucy said, "Hey Ben, nice to meet you. Wow, you're a good-looking guy, it's a great pity you aren't a female," Lucy said, laughing.

Ben said, "Ah, your, is this your girlfriend, Lucy?"

Lucy went to offer an answer, but the girl answered first, "Yes, it is. I'm Amy; nice to meet you."

Lucy looked at Amy, shocked but pleased with a smile at the same time. Then, Lucy said, "Yes, this is my girlfriend, Amy."

I said, "Pleased to meet you both." I saw Jake and Joe. I didn't know Joe had a wife, but apparently, she was to appear after work. Jake took an instant shine to Zoe when I introduced her, it's not surprising; she is beautiful. Jake said to me, "she is well out of my league, man."

I replied, "Hey, never say never, Man."

Daniel then says to the audience, "The day progressed nicely; we had arranged some games to play in the garden to keep the guests amused throughout the day. I had also invited some special guests, some of my acquaintances from a psycho-sexual clinic, which I had been affiliated to a couple of years before, this was mainly to accommodate Ben and Zoe as they had expressed an interest in the deviations of this world. We shall now look at an excerpt from Zoe's diary:

Dear Diary, we played games in the garden throughout the day, the first one was hilarious. There were four teams with ten people, standing one behind the other, in each team. Each team got a cucumber; in the first round, each person had to grasp the cucumber between their legs and pass it to the person in front of them, but you were only allowed to use your legs, no hands. Once the cucumber reached the last member of the team, they turned around and did the same operation in reverse. I had Jake behind me, and John in front of me when it was Jake's turn to pass the cucumber to me, he said, laughing, "Sorry, Zoe, this might hurt a bit."

I had a big smile on my face and said, "Oh, goody." I had the cucumber grasped firmly between my thighs as I turned around to John, "Okay, John, bend over and take it like a man," I said, laughing.

John said, "Ha, ha! Come here, you," he couldn't wait to get his hands on my shoulders and his thighs as close to mine as they were ever likely to get. I was wearing a little white cocktail dress, very short. "Okay, got it, Zoe," he said as he shuffled around to pass the cucumber on to the next person.

Once that game was over, each winner would get a shot of alcohol: this was their prize for winning. We were to stay in the same teams and positions for the following games. I'm not sure who was more pleased about that, Jake or John. A short time after the next game was to be played, each team got a cocktail sausage. Yes, you guessed it, Diary, we had to pass it to each other down the line using only our teeth with our hands behind our backs. I'm not sure who was more excited about this, Jake or John, I said laughing, "Right you two, behave, no tongues."

Jake and John were both laughing at this remark. John said, "I will try, Zoe."

"The pool is just over there, John," I said, laughing.

John said, "Okay, Zoe, I get the idea."

As the day progressed, there were other games, like transferring a tennis ball while using only your chin and neck. Another one was a balloon instead of a cucumber transferred from one set of thighs to another. It was all great fun.

Daniel then addresses the audience, "At this point, we shall take a short break; refreshments are available across the corridor in the other hall; please feel free to help yourselves; we shall resume in around twenty minutes."

After around twenty minutes, the hall began to fill up again. Once the hall was nearly full, Dr Daniel Brown made his way to the podium in the centre of the stage and began to speak:

"As I said earlier, the barbecue was held mainly to allow Ben and Zoe to meet some of their peers and to experience some of the deviations which they had expressed interest in before. After the games, everyone began to mingle and get acquainted in the various parts of the garden. I shall now present an excerpt from Ben's diary:"

Hey, Book, how are you doing? Well, that was an eventful day, to say the least, while I was chatting away to my good lady, Jo, I heard Zoe shout over to Daniel, "Hey Daniel,

Walter and I are going to have 'Sex on the Beach,' would you like to join us?"

Lisa burst into fits of laughter. Some of the other guests just looked in total surprise. I can only guess that they had never heard of that particular cocktail before. Daniel shouted back, "No thanks, Zoe, I have had a cocktail already."

A few of the older guests breathed a sigh of relief; most of them saw the funny side and just laughed. Shortly after, John came over and said, "Hey, Ben, I think I've actually pulled. I looked across to where he had been sitting at one of the bar stands. From where I was standing, it looked like a very pretty blonde lady was waiting for him to return to her. Just at that, my mobile vibrated, it was a text from Daniel, it read, 'Hey, Ben, don't say anything to John but the pretty lady he is chatting up is Alexis, used to be Alexander a short while ago.'"

I just laughed a little and said, "Well done, John!"

As Daniel was passing by them, Alexis said, "Hi, Dr Brown, how are you?"

Daniel said, "Yes, I'm fine, thanks; are you the full Alexis yet?"

The answer was, "Not quite yet, Dr Brown, just one more little snip, and we're there," Alexis said, laughing.

Daniel said, "Please, call me, Daniel."

"Okay, Daniel, since I'm not all the way there yet, you can call me Alex," she said, laughing.

John said, "Sorry, I think I've lost the train of this conversation."

"He shouldn't worry about it, should he, Daniel?" said Alex.

"No, John, nothing to worry about," said Daniel. John went back over to Alex and continued chatting away. I continued my conversation with Jo.

Daniel then addresses the audience, "Ben and Zoe both got to meet Alex later in the day. They both agreed what a nice person she was. Alex told John the truth about his impending sex change." John just said, "That's a pity as we got on so well, but don't take offence by this, but we won't be pursuing a relationship, however, I wish you all the best for the future."

At another bar stand, Jake was sitting on his own. Zoe went over and said, "Hey, Cowboy, how are you doing?"

Jake replied, "Darling and Cowboy, all on the same day. I don't know if I can handle all these compliments," he said, laughing.

"Tell me about yourself, Jake."

"Sure," Jake said, "I'm 29 years old, a qualified mechanic, single, never been married, but had a few girlfriends, but nothing serious. What about you, Zoe?"

Zoe said, "Well, I'm 45."

Jake said, "Yeah, right."

Zoe said, "Sorry, I mean, I'm 25. I work in a hardware store. I'm single at the moment."

Jake said, laughing, "Given the events of the day so far, I take it you never used to be a man?"

Zoe said, "Not at all; can I also say, I take it you never used to be a woman?" Zoe then said, "Jake, do you not find some of the deviations in this world fascinating"?

Jake said, "In this world, how many worlds have you been to, kid?"

Zoe said, "Sorry, I mean in the world."

Jake said, "Hell, yeah, see that guy over there, he used to be a she. I was speaking to her/him earlier."

Zoe said, "I understand how a man could change into a woman with the surgery, but how could a woman function as a man?"

Jake said, "It's still surgery, but it's a case of an attachment rather than a detachment if you know what I mean?"

Zoe says, "But how could it work within a union, I mean, in a relationship."

Jake said, "Well, to my knowledge, it isn't great, but I did see a TV programme about that sort of stuff once, and I did ask that question because I was curious as well. Apparently, there are various options, but in that guy's particular case, it was a pump you attach to the male formed bit and pump it up when required, but I'm told that this is an extreme version of the sex change."

Zoe said, "Well, I am totally shocked to hear this. It sounds more like a machine than a person."

A guy just then appeared and said, "Hi, guys, have any of you seen Joe around?"

Jake said, "He's around somewhere, man. I'm Jake. I work with Joe; are you one of his mates?"

"Well, kind of. I'm Ken. I'm Joe's wife; nice to meet you all."

Zoe had just taken a mouthful of cocktail but spurted it out at this revelation, "You're his wife, but you're such a good-looking guy, and so is Joe."

Ken said, "Thank you, it is what it is. I'll go find him."

After Ken left, the two, Jake and Zoe, both looked at one another in disbelief. Jake said, "Well, I never knew Joe was gay."

Zoe said, "What a couple of good-looking guys to be that way inclined, but I suppose it takes all sorts. I take it you're not that way inclined, Jake?" Zoe said.

Jake replied, "Not at all, Kiddo, what you see is what you get. I know I'm not that pretty, but I'm a full-blooded, heterosexual male."

I told Jake that that was good to hear, considering the events of the day. I said to Ben later that day, "I wonder what the teacher would have made of all this, Ben? I've met a man who used to be a woman; a woman that used to be a man; men that dress and portray themselves as women; women that dress and portray themselves as men; A two female relationship; a two male relationship. This truly is a fascinating world compared to our simple home world where men are men and women are women."

Ben replied, "It sure is a different world, Kiddo."

Daniel then addressed the audience, "So, it is becoming apparent that although Zoe and Ben were fascinated with the deviations and different inter-personal relationships in this world, it is a lot for them to accept when they are so used to the simplicity that is their own society."

I had a rather interesting conversation with Ben the other night. I would like to share with you the diary entry which he wrote afterward; here is an excerpt from Ben's diary:

Hey, Book, how are you doing? Yet another interesting day in this new world and a very interesting conversation with

Daniel this evening. I had said, "Daniel, can I ask you a question?"

"Of course, Ben, what can I help you with?"

"Okay, last year, you deduced that the universe was infinite, Daniel, and that black holes were actually quantum singularities to accommodate the infinite nature of the universe, yes?"

"Yes, Ben."

"Daniel, have you ever considered that the black holes, as well as being quantum singularities, may also be connections to other universes. In fact, an infinite number of universes?"

Daniel replied, "Now, that is a theory, Ben, and a quite possible one, however not one, which we can prove or disprove at this moment in time. Pretty much the same as the infinite universe theory, although in that case, an infinite universe is the only logical explanation."

I said to Daniel that I had taken his point, then asked him what he thought of the Zoe and Jake situation.

Daniel said, laughing, "So long as Zoe is happy, it wasn't something which I had expected, but you never know what's around that corner, Ben."

Daniel then says to the audience, "Perhaps, I should explain this portion of the excerpt from Ben's diary. I think the best way would be to look at another excerpt from Zoe's diary:"

Dear, Diary, where shall I start with this bit? Okay, when we were at Daniel and Lisa's barbecue, I met Jake, a new workmate of Ben's. My first impression was that he was a very big man with a big shaggy beard. Jake wasn't what I would call good-looking, but at the same time, he wasn't what I would call ugly, not that I would ever call anyone ugly because that's rude. As the day progressed at the barbecue, and the more I got chatting to Jake, the more I felt at ease with him, as the drinks flowed; Jake obviously liked me; he had made that quite clear. I looked into his eyes, and I could see no harm there. I said, "Jake, you know what, I will be with you."

Jake said, "What do you mean, Zoe?"

I said, "In a union."

Jake said, "Zoe, Kiddo. I don't think we can be in the same union. I'm in the mechanics union; you're a sales assistant; different unions, Kiddo."

"Jake," I said, "you misunderstood. I meant I will be with you."

Jake said, "Yeah, okay. I will be with you too, Kiddo."

Daniel says to the audience, "If you remember from the lecture last year, this is how these species form relationships with the simple phrase, I will be with you, if it is reciprocated, they become a couple. We shall now return to Zoe's diary:"

I said to Jake, "Well, I really do look forward to our first encounter."

Jake looked a bit puzzled and said, "Kiddo, I'm a bit confused; what are you actually saying, Zoe?"

I said, "Sorry, Jake, it's a little thing we do where I come from, if I say I will be with you and you say it back, we are, then a couple, if you are okay with that, Jake?"

Jake yelled, "Fuck, yeah, sorry, I mean hell yeah," Jake was stuttering, saying, "aww, Zoe, you won't be disappointed, I promise you."

I said, "I'm sure I won't, Darling."

Jake said, "Stay here, don't move, Kiddo. I'll be back in two minutes." Jake ran over to another stand where Ben, Joe, and Ken were chatting. I couldn't hear what was said, but from Jake's actions, it was like he was telling them that he had just won the lottery.

Ben said to me later, "Zoe, you have just made that guy the happiest man on this planet. I hope it goes well for you both."

I said to Ben, laughing, "Ben, I already know how it's going, and it is going great. Jake isn't the best-looking guy on the planet, but oh boy, he has got experience with the opposite sex and Boy has he got stamina."

Ben was laughing and said, "Well, Kid, you don't waste any time, do you?"

I said, "It has been rather a while since my last union, Ben."

Ben said, "I'm so happy for you, Zoe. I'm getting on great with Jo as well, but we're still taking it easy as it comes."

I said, "That's great, Ben, best way."

Dr Daniel Brown then addresses the audience and says, "We will now take a short break; tea, coffee, light refreshments, and sandwiches are available in the hall opposite. Please feel free to help yourselves; we shall resume in around twenty minutes."

After around twenty minutes, the hall started to fill up again. When everyone was seated, Daniel made his way to the podium in the centre of the stage and began to speak:

"Okay, so we can see that the barbecue was a resounding success. Everyone had a great time, especially Ben and Zoe. They had expressed an interest in the deviations that exist in this world, and I did my very best to accommodate them by introducing them to various individuals whom I had encountered during one of my secondments. We can now see that the dynamics of the scenario have changed slightly, as Ben is now with Jo; Zoe is now with Jake. We discovered that Joe and Ken were married, which none of Joe's workmates knew before. Lucy now has a new girlfriend, which I am not sure whether she was expecting when the question was asked, but we wish them all the best. As I said earlier, there would be a time for questions at the end of the lecture, and sadly, we are here. It has been most enjoyable this year to see you all again, and I trust, you will all take something relevant away from this lecture. In the meantime, does anyone have any questions they would like to ask me?"

Professor Rona Graham raised her hand and said, "Dr Brown, can I ask, did John manage to find a girlfriend at the barbecue?"

Dr Brown replied, "Unfortunately, not, although John was getting on famously with Alexis, once he found out she used to be Alexander, that was the end of that potential relationship. John didn't manage to find another lady who he liked at the barbecue, so, unfortunately, John is still looking for the right Mrs John." Then, Dr Brown says, laughing, "can I ask, are you interested in John, Professor Graham?"

Rona replied, "No, Sir, I was just curious to see if he managed to find love yet."

Dan said, "No, he's still looking, Professor Graham."

Dan asked, "Any more questions?"

Dr Clive Durham raised his hand and said, "Dr Brown, how possible do you personally think it is that there are multiple or even infinite universes like Ben said?"

Daniel said, "The best way I can answer that is that a few hundred years ago, Man believed that the world was flat and if we sailed too far, we would fall off the edge; now, we have progressed to possess far more knowledge. The deduction that the universe is, in fact, infinite does leave the door open for the theory which Ben presented that there are, in fact, infinite universes which, obviously, at this moment in time, we cannot prove nor disprove, so it must remain a theory."

Dr Mary Reynolds raised her hand and said, "How do you feel, Dr Brown, about Zoe entering into a relationship with Jake; do you not think it is all a bit soon for her?"

Daniel said, "Well, I know Zoe quite well now, and I trust her judgment if she believes that Jake is a suitable partner for her. It is not my place to say any different."

Professor Craig Arnold raised his hand and said, "Dr Brown, with this race having superior morality and honesty values, how does that fit into Ben's relationship with Jo."

Dr Brown said, "If you are referring to the lack of commitment within their relationship, there is no dishonesty there. Ben has been totally honest with Jo to say that he was not ready to commit to a full relationship. Jo is quite happy with the situation, so I fail to see any problem, as there is no breach of morality or honesty by either party."

Dr Hans Schneider raised his hand and said, "Dr Brown, do you not think the authorities should be notified, concerning the origins of the Coronavirus?"

Daniel replied, "Absolutely not! We are all bound by the Official Secrets Act not to repeat anything that is divulged within this or any other lecture. Furthermore, Zoe volunteered to relay the information in good faith and confidence, a trust which I would not dream of breaking, also as we said earlier, we do not have the technology to find this race in space, and even if we did, why should we compound a situation with a further assault when it was ourselves who initiated the first act of aggression. So, no, the authorities will not be notified by me or anyone within this lecture; you are all bound by the Official Secrets Act, the penalty for breaching it is life imprisonment."

Dr Daniel Brown then says to the audience, "If there are no more questions, I apologise for ending the lecture on such a harsh note, but it is an extremely serious situation. I would like to thank you all for attending this year, and I trust you all have enjoyed this lecture. I wish you all well and have a safe journey home. Thank you!"

The audience gave Daniel a standing ovation with loud cheers that lasted for a few minutes. When the noise began to subside, Daniel bowed and said without the microphone, "Thank you, thank you!" As Dr Daniel Brown made his way to the exit of the auditorium, he felt his eyes filling up; this had been an extremely emotional lecture for all concerned and mentioned.

Daniel got to his car and put the roof down with the touch of a button. It was a beautiful evening as Daniel drove the twenty-five miles to his home. When Daniel reached home, he went into the kitchen, where Lisa was preparing their evening meal. Dan went right over and gave her a big kiss and a cuddle with a huge sigh of relief.

"How did it go, Honey?" Lisa asked.

Daniel replied, "Yes, I think it went very well, Babes, I'm going…."

Lisa interrupted, "To go down to the garage to unwind a bit before dinner."

"Yes," Daniel was laughing, "you know me so well, dear, give me a shout when dinner's ready, yeah?"

"Okay, Honey, will do," Lisa replied.

As Daniel made his way through their large garden, he remembered what a great day it had been at the barbecue, how Zoe had met Jake and started a union, how everyone had enjoyed themselves and Dan had a little snigger, as he thought how John had behaved himself. It was a great day.

As Daniel entered his large garage, he saw the sub-frame of his kit car in the centre of the floor. He remembered how Ben had been such a great help to him in building it. Daniel sat on his workbench and began to look through the plans for the car. As he did so, he started laughing; in the top left-hand corner of one of the sheets was a smiley face and three kisses with a Z beside them.

Daniel said, laughing, "Zoe," as he shook his head. Daniel's thoughts then went back to the lecture and to the day of the barbecue. Dan smiled and thought how he missed Zoe and Ben popping up unexpectedly now and again. Dan pulled his mobile out of his pocket and said, "call, Ben." The phone started to ring. After a few seconds, it was answered.

"Hey, how are you doing?"

Daniel said, "Hi, Ben," but the voice continued, "I must be busy because I haven't answered; when you hear the beep, you know what to do, catch ya soon."

Daniel didn't say anything; he just pressed the end call sign on his phone. Dan thought to himself, *well, that's a first.*

Ben has always answered before. Daniel put his head in his hands and thought how he missed the two being around. Lisa came into the garage at that point and said, "You, okay, Honey?"

Dan replied, "Yeah, just reflecting on a few things, Babes."

"Are you missing Ben and Zoe being around, Honey?"

Daniel replied, "I am a bit, Babes, but it is what it is."

Lisa said, "Give Ben a call."

Dan replied, "I just did, Babes, went onto the answering machine." "To hell with it. I'll try Zoe," Dan said. He said to his phone, "call Zoe."

The phone replied, "Calling Zoe." After a few seconds, the phone started to ring, "Hello, hello, this is Zoe, well, it's a recording of me, if you'd like to leave a message, I'll call you back, thank you!"

Again, Daniel didn't say anything; he just pressed end call. Lisa said, "They'll call back later, Babes, I'll go serve dinner, you ready for it?"

"Yeah, I'm starving," said Daniel, "let's go." Just as they left the garage, Daniel's mobile rang, he looked and saw Ben's name on the screen. Daniel answered his phone quickly, "Ben, how are you doing?"

"Hey, Danny boy, I'm cool, cool. How are you, my friend?"

Daniel replied, "Yes, Ben, I'm good; cheers."

"Sorry, I missed your call. I was at the pool," Ben said.

"No worries," said Daniel.

"How do you fancy us working on your car tomorrow, Daniel? It's Saturday. and I'm not working, so I have all day free."

"That would be great, Ben," Daniel said.

Ben replied, "Cool, I'll be over just after breakfast."

Dan said, "Great, Ben, see you then."

After Dan had ended the call with Ben, a few seconds later, his phone rang again, "Zoe, how are you doing?"

"I'm good, thank you, Daniel! Is Lisa there, please?"

"Yes. Sure, here she is."

After a few minutes, Lisa ended the call and said, "Well, that's my day sorted tomorrow. Zoe and I are going shopping and for lunch so, you can work on your car all day, Honey."

Daniel breathed a sigh of relief, "So, they haven't forgotten us after all, Babes."

Lisa said, laughing, "don't be silly, Honey, they'll never forget us…"

*Dr Daniel Brown, here. I do hope you have enjoyed this lecture and the diaries contained within it. I promise to keep you updated with Ben and Zoe's progress in their new lives here. Next year's lecture shall be rather different, but I won't say too much, as it will spoil it for you. I look forward to seeing you all again next year. I wish you well…